HERO

Written by Chloe Kent

Hello, again!

My fourth book. I can't quite believe it but I do know I'm enjoying it more with each one I write and I am so thankful to you for purchasing my latest story.

I need to give a huge thank you to Bailey McGinn for creating an awesome front cover and my editor, Fiona Watson, for editing my fourth book! It's with their help this book has come to life.

Also, a big thank you to my husband for his patience as always as I write until the early hours of the morning, a thank you to the girl group chat for reading along as I wrote and being an incredible support and as always, thank you to ELRY Agency, who are the best hype girls and team I could ever want.

Happy reading!

Love, Chloe xx

PROLOGUE

Everyone remembers exactly where they were or what they were doing on the morning of September 11th, 2001.

The moment the world was shaken by the biggest terror attack to date, the moment four planes were taken over by hijackers and purposely crashed in three different states in America, murdering nearly three thousand innocent people whilst the World helplessly watched.

Everyone remembers that moment because it changed them. It either changed the way they saw the World, or it changed their own World, and nothing would ever be the same again.

Dawson Caine, an off-duty firefighter, was asleep in his bed following a typical nightshift at the New York Fire Department when he was awoken by the phone ringing on the nightstand. It was 8:54am, approximately eight minutes after the first plane had hit the north tower. The call was from his wife Kimberly, who was a receptionist for a large insurance company on the 92nd floor.

Dawson answered the phone to his frantic and terrified wife; he heard her sobs and cries over loud crashing and banging in the background. He pressed his ear hard against the receiver, trying to make sense of her words. Eventually, Kimberly took a breath and clearly explained.

"Dawson, baby, listen. I saw it. A huge plane, it hit the building. I think it's two or three floors above me. I thought I could get out, but the elevator has blown. I can't get to the stairs, there's debris and smoke everywhere. I'm going to die here. I know it, I'm going to die here. Please know that becoming your wife and having our son has been my greatest achievements in life... Oh god, my baby Hendrix. Tell him I love him so very much. I love you. I love you baby..."

The call disconnected and Dawson was immediately in the

car and on his way to the fire department to get suited up, despite the station manager pleading with him to stay on the ground.

"Daws, don't do it man, you're far too emotional, you'll be no good up there. Stay here. They'll find her, just stay here." – Station manager

"I can't do that. That's my wife up there." – Dawson Caine

Those were the last words of Firefighter Dawson Caine. Twenty-three minutes after he entered the building, the North Tower completely collapsed. Dawson's and Kimberly's bodies were never found.

When school finished that day, eight-year-old Hendrix would learn that both his parents were gone. He was picked up by a social worker before being transferred to Rhode Island to live the rest of his childhood with his Grandma Josephine. As soon as Hendrix celebrated his eighteenth birthday, he enlisted into the Marines.

CHAPTER ONE

HENDRIX

"You know, it's been almost six months and I really hoped that we would be making real progress by now." She gives me the one-arched eyebrow frown, the same she always has when she grows restless with me.

I told her eleven months ago that I didn't want to talk; if I wasn't under some shitty court order, I wouldn't even be here in the first place. Therapy is not my thing.

"There's nothing to say." I shrug, carelessly.

Her eyes narrow onto me and she leans forward, her arms crossed on her lap.

"Nothing to say? Hendrix Caine, you are a thirty-year-old man, you have no parents, no siblings and you've been invited to leave your career by the U.S Marines, and you have nothing to say about any of that? You're here because it was this or prison. At the very least I'm going to need some information on why that is if I'm to let the court know that you're not a danger to anyone else."

My jaw twitches at the last part, she knows that's my Achilles heel. I'd sooner be back in some dusty ass desert in the middle of nowhere being shot at than sitting here on this pretentious brown leather couch being judged by some snobby sheltered suburban chick whose only difficulty in life is choosing what colour nail polish to get at the salon that week.

"Okay, fine, I'll rephrase: there is nothing I *want* to say." I smirk just a little as she frowns deeper at my reply.

She shuffles restlessly in her green armchair before picking up the clipboard from the little coffee table beside her. Her eyes flicker up and down the checklist as she removes the plastic lid from her biro.

"Are you taking the pills I prescribed?"

I nod.

"Are you sleeping through the night?"

I nod again, ignoring the fact that most nights I need a few whiskeys on ice to send me to sleep properly. Last time I didn't, I woke up in a cold sweat from a thunderstorm but in my dreams the thunder were bombs going over my head.

"And you remember I told you that you can't consume alcohol on those particular pills, right?"

"Yep."

"Remember how we spoke about the importance of socialising last week? How's that going?"

"I fucked a chick in the parking lot of a Wendy's at the weekend, does that count?"

She scribbles something down aggressively, so I'm guessing it doesn't.

"I'd like to take you back to the fight you had with fellow Marine Martinez…"

"Fuck him." I cut her off instantly. "I'm not talking about him."

"You say that every time, but he is a lot of why you're here."

I can't conceal my anxiety and I sigh heavily at the memory, so much so, it prompts Dr Edwards to scribble more bullshit down.

"It was this or prison, remember? That's why I'm here," I answer restlessly.

"Right, then let's discuss that part. Why didn't you go to prison? Why did he drop those charges? My report says that you put him in a bad way…"

I roll my eyes, annoyed by the sympathetic tone in her voice as if Martinez is some victim.

"The guy fucking deserved it."

"He deserved a broken nose?"

I nod, trying not to get sucked into the memory again but she lists off all his injuries as if I'm unaware of what I did. Each description brings on this anxiety, it's a horrible feeling that I can't control – my body goes tingly and all heavy, like I can't pick myself up and my brain starts to wander back to the past...

"He had a fractured jaw, a fractured eye socket, he lost several teeth... the list goes on, but let's not forget the ruptured spleen that almost killed him..."

Her voice begins to fade out and become muffled, like she's talking to me from under water; the black mist clouds my eyes and I brace myself as my body goes completely numb and my mind throws me straight back into the same fucking flashbacks that I've been trying to avoid.

I'm back there. The heat beats down on the back of my neck; the weight of my rifle which I've been carrying all day is pulling me down, making me feel heavier and tired. I'm on my own because I had heard a scream that I had to follow. With every step I hear it again, a blood-curdling scream. I drag my feet and my heavy combat boots through the rocky gravel, following the sound. I approach a row of tiny concrete houses which should be abandoned, but with every step closer it's obvious that someone must have been left behind. I raise my gun as I close in on the entrance. I take one last inhale before stepping inside, my gun up high, ready for whatever I'm about to be challenged with.

"Aye! It's Caine! One minute bud, you'll have to get in line – when I'm done with her, it's Avery's turn."

I can hear my heart thumping in my ears. My eyes dart to Avery who has a satanic smile across his face as he waits at the side, his belt already unbuckled. He winks before turning his attention back – back to watching Martinez rape a civilian. Sweat drips into my eyes and I squeeze them tightly, praying that when I re-open them I'll see that it wasn't what I thought. I squeeze them twice, but when I re-open them the image is the same. A young woman, no older than twenty, is bent over a shabby wooden table with her dress pulled up high above her hips; her bloodied face is pressed against the table, tears causing her dark brown hair to stick to her cheek. She looks up at me, timidly, but her eyes are pleading for help. Her petite body is trembling beneath the weight of a thug who was sent here to protect her. I stare at Martinez, my buddy, someone I had thought was a good guy. He uses his bloodied fist – a fist he has clearly already to hit her with - to grab her by her hair and make her scream in pain.

"Yeah! She likes it rough!"

Suddenly, the images flash again but this time making sense. Her bloodied face, his bloodied fist, her tears, his trousers dropped to his ankles, her cries, his laugh…

And then I don't know. It's all a blur. The next thing I know I'm standing over Martinez watching him drift into unconsciousness as blood pools around him. The girl climbs to her feet, using the back of her hand to wipe her tears. Avery runs off like the coward he is. The girl gives me a look of appreciation before disappearing and I'm left alone with what I assume is a dead Marine. I watch his eyes glaze over before his lids drop shut, the blood spreads until it's almost at my feet, I stare at Martinez, the man I called my best friend and I feel sick, I watch him, hoping that he doesn't take another breath. Then something else, a loud rumble, a plane, a firefighter climbing up to the 92nd floor to rescue the woman he could never save. Then a small boy, waiting for Mom and Dad after school, waiting and waiting, but he's alone until one day he struggles to even remember their faces. He cries himself to sleep most nights, he writes letters to Santa and asks him if he can bring back his parents. He cowers over whenever he hears the sound of a plane. Inside he is broken. The boy is me. My body begins shaking uncontrollably and it seems to jolt me back into the present.

"Hendrix, Hendrix… can you hear me?"

Dr Edwards is fanning me with her clipboard; she studies me carefully as I blink the black mist away and come back from the dark visions that scare the hell out of me.

"I think you had a panic attack…" she announces but sounding unsure.

"No shit," I croak, my throat dry as hell. Sweat beads drip from my forehead.

"Do you want to stop for today?"

I shake my head. She wants the truth so bad.

"Dr Edwards, the reason I am here is because Martinez couldn't press those charges. If he had, it would have gone to court, and I would have had to tell everyone that the reason I beat the shit out of him is because he is a filthy dirty rapist who gets off on innocent women crying for him to stop being the animal he is. And if I had killed him, I could have lived with it."

CHAPTER TWO

MADDISON

My two blonde best friends giggle as they clink their peach Bellinis and squeal with excitement whilst they announce all the exciting highlights from their itinerary.

"Oh my god! Wait! We have a New Orleans visit too!" Hannah gasps as her smile lights up her face. She has the biggest smile, it has always reminded me of Julia Roberts, it is easily her best feature. Hannah is gorgeous – she has long blonde wavy hair and piercing blue eyes. It's like Julia Roberts and the mermaid from *Splash* had a love child.

Poppy looks at her confused. "Am I supposed to know what that means?"

Hannah glances at me and rolls her eyes. We joke on occasion that Poppy tends to remind us of Karen from *Mean Girls*. Looks wise though, she's very different – she pulls off her short haircut which she messes up with a little product and that's it, she's done, and it looks so cool. I could never pull off a look like that. It reminds me of Pink from her *So What* music video, just totally feisty and badass.

"It's the place famous for Mardi Gras, Pops," I inform her. Her eyes go wide as the penny drops.

"Oh my god! So it's party central then? This trip is going to be insane!"

They simultaneously knock back their Bellinis and use their empty flutes to air high-five in celebration. Poppy stares at me awkwardly and I realise my facial expressions must be giving away the FOMO I'm feeling inside.

"Shit, Mads, we don't mean to gloat..."

"It's not gloating if she's coming with us, is it!" Hannah interrupts her quickly and she shoots me a smile and winks.

I offer up a fake laugh which fools neither of them.

"I wish I could, but four weeks is a long time, and I don't think Jamie will go for it."

Hannah sighs restlessly. "Jeez Mads, Jamie isn't your dad you know."

Poppy reaches out and gives my hand a little squeeze.

"What Hannah means is, you're young, you only get one life – surely Jamie can let you go for one month to travel the states with your two best friends?"

I can picture Jamie already, shaking his head at the very idea. My shoulders instantly tense up just at the mere thought of the huge lecture I'd have to endure.

"You're right, he probably will. I'm just being silly."

"That's the spirit! Of course he'll let you go – he might be madly in love with you and I know he gets worried easily, but just reassure him that you're with us! We'll take care of each other." Poppy seems so sure of it and smiles sweetly; behind her, Hannah's expression is entirely different – she knows Poppy is wasting her breath. In front of my friends, Jamie presents as the nicest guy in the world. Hannah seems to be the only person who sees through it. I'm not saying Jamie is bad, he's just… Jamie.

I'm not sure when I became the friend who lets everyone down, but that is all I seem to do now. I couldn't go to Hannah's older sister's hen night because the request was that we all dress up in a silly costume from Ann Summers, like a sexy nurse or a bunny, something outrageous, tacky and fun. Everything a hen party usually is. Then at the very last minute, when my costume was on and I was nearly out the door, I had to listen to a forty-five-minute lecture from Jamie about how my outfit was inappropriate and I was massively letting myself down. He listed off all the ways that I had cheapened myself to appease my friends and how when I'm out of the house I represent us as a couple, and he doesn't want anyone thinking he is dating a slapper.

A few years back, before we met, Jamie's dad passed away and left him *a lot* of money. With it, he opened his own gym and within eight months he had opened three more. Although Jamie doesn't like it when I call them gyms – he prefers the term *Private Members Health Club*. It's more than a gym you see. A gym implies anyone can attend, but Jamie's Health Club is far pickier with its clientele. Only well-established, upper-class people are able to join. I prefer a gym that plays Cardi B telling me all about her WAP when I'm working out, but those days are over. In fact, Jamie doesn't like me listening to a lot of music. He says Cardi B is vulgar and an embarrassment to women and anyone who listens to her must be the dregs of society without a single brain cell. Jamie and I have been together almost a year and I swear he wasn't always this way. Well, I don't think he was. He has always been a bit of a chauvinist, but I assumed it was just banter – until it got worse.

For my birthday I treated myself to a tattoo of a cherry blossom branch across the top of my shoulder. I was so happy with it. Three hours I sat in that chair like a pro, barely squinting in pain even though inside I was screaming. I'm a wimp, what can I say? I practically skipped home I was so excited to show Jamie. I had images playing out in my head of him finding me irresistible and wanting to rip off my clothes. I genuinely thought we'd be fully getting naked on his kitchen table whilst he admired the artwork on my body. Instead, he gawped at me in disbelief before ringing my own mother up to tell her what I had done. My mum has never been a fan of tattoos or piercings, she firmly believes ink is for paper and not our bodies, so she was utterly disappointed. I'm not sure which was worse – my mother moaning on the phone that she was worried about what her friends would think when they saw me, or Jamie telling me he didn't want to make love to me for a while he tried to get used to it.

I went to bed that night feeling embarrassed and stupid. Whilst Jamie huffed and stomped around the apartment in a bad mood, I sat on the edge of the bed staring at myself in the floor length mirror in front of me. I admired my chocolate brown hair that draped over my shoulders and stared at my hazel eyes and my long eyelashes – they have always been my favourite feature about myself. My eyes scanned my creamy ivory skin (which, come to think of it, could really use some sun). I'm quite short, around five foot four, which means I'm rubbish at carrying any extra pounds – they go straight to my hips and give my stomach a little pouch. I don't usually mind, mostly because I follow a hundred body positive Instagram accounts that have been drumming into me that I have a beautiful curvy womanly shape and that I should be grateful for all this incredible body does for me.

Jamie suddenly appeared from the steamy bathroom like a contestant from *Stars in Their Eyes*, only he was half naked with a grey towel wrapped around his waist, his newly highlighted blond hair in a damp shaggy mop, bringing out his green eyes.

"Babe, maybe watch the carbs for the next week or so," he said, so casually, as he nodded towards the little roll on my stomach.

I nodded and forced a smile, casually brushing off the words as if they caused me no offence.

***

I lay in bed that night staring up at the ceiling, thinking about me and Jamie, thinking about our future. My family love him, my mum mostly. She thinks Jamie is the best thing since sliced bread, but I know why, deep down. It's his money. Now I'm not saying my mum is a gold digger, but she didn't come from much and she has always wanted more for me. I guess in her way she thinks Jamie will make me happy and give me a security that she never had. Dad leaving didn't help. He left Mum for a woman half his age that he met at work and now he lives with her in Dublin, leaving me behind in Berkshire to pick up the pieces.

I wake up with the sun streaming through Jamie's new venetian blinds and I've made my decision. I want to wear cowboy boots in Tennessee and sunbathe in the Florida Keys, I want to drink Margaritas in New Orleans – but mostly, I want to be happy again. I've been losing my spark for months now, and I want the old Maddison back. I need this adventure more than I realised. I have woken up and never felt surer that I need to do this for myself.

I plan to cook a special (but of course healthy) meal for when Jamie gets home from work – salmon and vegetables and for afters a summery Eton Mess with natural yogurt instead of cream and a huge jug of icy lemon water on the table. It'll be perfect. Then, when he's nice and relaxed, I'll mention the trip with the girls and explain how good it will be for me. He might not get it at first, but by the end of the meal, I know he'll understand that this is important to me. Relationships are all about compromise. I work fifty hours a week as a receptionist in the first health club he opened, on minimum wage because he says he needs to concentrate on putting money elsewhere right now, and I have never argued with that. Surely, if I can do that, he can put up with one month without me.

CHAPTER THREE

HENDRIX

I have never visited Ground Zero and the memorial for the victims of that day, ever. I know my parents' names are inscribed on bronze parapets because my grandmother visited many times, and she told me. She offered plenty of times to take me to the spot, so that I could see it with my own eyes, but the very thought of stepping into Manhattan was too much. I was just a kid then, there is no way I could stand in the same spot where both my parents were killed.

Since leaving the Marines, I have managed to visit New York a couple of times, but I can only make it as far as the fire station where my dad worked – I have never been inside. My grandma said that they have their own memorial in there for him too. On the plaque, they call him 'Dawson Hero Caine' because he came back to rescue my mom. The story goes that although he never reached my mom, he did manage to save eleven people trapped on the 83rd floor, including a young woman who was eight months pregnant. The tower fell seconds after she made it out. She came to the funeral and gave a speech where she called my dad her hero. She went on to have a healthy baby boy, and she named him David-Dawson. My grandma cried when she heard. I don't remember meeting her at the funeral but there are plenty of photos that tell me otherwise. That entire day was a blur really. I don't think about it much.

The sheer volume of taxis beeping and people hollering at one another snaps me into the present. I'm back again. I know I can't make it anywhere near Ground Zero, but it doesn't stop me from trying. It's bright and early, almost nine in the morning, and there's not a cloud in the sky, just like it was on the morning of the 11th. I check back on Google Maps, I'm a thirteen-minute walk from Ground Zero. I stare up to the skyline momentarily and a flash of a plane crashing into the North Tower pierces my brain and startles me. It's enough for me to move out of the sidewalk and hover by a shop for security instead. My heart begins thumping, my chest gets tight and my hands tingle. If I don't walk away now, I'm going to have a fucking episode.

"You were in the fucking Marines Hendrix, you can do this," I mumble to myself, but it comes out angry and I know that's because I already know deep down that I'm done.

I take a few steps forward when I see a small Irish bar.

"Fuck it." I take solace inside; I order a double whiskey on ice and hang my head over my glass in shame. I can feel the sweat running down my back, proving to me that I was about to end up as a heap of anxiety on the sidewalk.

"Rough day?" the red-haired barmaid pipes up. She stinks of stale cigarettes and grease. I barely make eye contact with her; I concentrate on the ice swimming in my favourite brown liquor that burns my throat just as well as it burns the memories from my head. For a while anyway.

"Not really up for making friends today, if you don't mind." I pick up my glass and knock back my drink in one; the burn drops down into my chest and I feel relieved. "I'll have another."

I slide my glass across the bar to her and although I don't look up, I can sense she's smiling. If she thinks I'm about to fuck her she's eight whiskeys too early.

Four whiskeys later and the memories that were haunting me out on the street have been burned away but the anger inside me is still there, with no place to go.

"So, what's this tattoo mean?"

I peer down and see the barmaid's hand tapping my knuckle.

"I have a lot of tattoos, this'll be a long conversation and I'm not nearly drunk enough."

She grins, showing her tobacco-stained teeth and pours another whiskey into my glass.

"That one's on the house baby, now tell me about the tattoo."

The tattoo she's referring to starts at my knuckles and finishes at my wrist. It says, amid a lot of shading, *till death* and below it is a pair of playing cards, a king and a queen. It's a nod to my parents who were each other's world and loved each other till the very end. I mean, fuck, my dad climbed ninety stair wells to save his soul mate, no wonder it made a lot of news outlets and documentaries since. But I'm not about to tell red-head that. It's none of her business.

"Saw it in an artist's portfolio, liked it, got it, that's it."

She doesn't seem at all phased by the blatant lack of conversation I'm offering up.

"What about this one?" She jabs her finger onto my throat, disregarding my personal space and beginning to piss me off.

"American eagle," I answer flatly and gesture for another shot.

She fills my glass again, her eyes staying on me.

"What's below it? I can see more poking out."

"Wings, scripture, roses, things like that. Like I said, I have a lot."

"Cool, I like the sound of that. Fancy coming out back and showing me?"

Here we go.

She stares at me with hope. And I stare back with disgust.

Which I absolutely didn't mean to do, but she's clocked my reaction and she's looking mad as hell.

"What's that fucking look for?" she asks, her voice all high-pitched and offended.

But before I even have a second to answer she's fully going off on me.

"You'd be lucky to have someone like me – who the hell else would want some drunk on a Monday morning? Asshole."

"Sure. I'm an asshole." I shrug my shoulders, not really giving

a shit.

"Where you from anyhow, jerk? I haven't seen you in here

before. What's your name?"

"Hendrix. Hendrix Caine."

The words come but my lips didn't move. I quickly realise the voice came from behind me. Somebody from this bar must know me, somebody was able to answer for me.

I spin on my bar stool to see an old man, grey hair, sleeked back, looking like he started his morning looking smart, but now, the booze is definitely kicking his ass harder than it is mine.

"Do I know you, sir?" I ask, standing up from my stool.

"I knew your dad and you're the spitting image of him. We worked together for some time; I met you a couple of times too, but you were just a kid..."

He laughs like he recalls some amusing memory but his whole demeanour is off.

"Hero? That's what they called him right?" he asks rhetorically.

My hands slide into my pockets, hiding the balled-up fists that have formed. The way he said Hero was off, like he tasted something revolting and wanted to spit it out.

"So they tell me sir."

"Tell me son, what hero ignores instruction from his colleagues and the station manager to stay on the ground? What hero risks his life knowing he could cause his son to be an orphan? What hero drags colleagues up to the 90th floor to help him, only to die instead..."

"That's enough, old timer," the barmaid surprisingly answers for me. She can obviously sense his tone is shitty just like I can.

He doesn't seem deterred; in fact, he continues. "He was no hero. He was selfish, self-centred, unprofessional and reckless."

I can feel the tension rushing to my fists. I smirk in his face, showing him that his words don't phase me, but inside I'm at boiling point.

"I'm warning you, old man. Watch your mouth."

"Oh, you're definitely Dawson's son all right. You have that 'I don't give a fuck' attitude. Nice. Although it didn't get your dad too far, did it?"

Black mist clouds my vision and my body tenses up. Within a split second my fist connects with his jaw, knocking him straight back over his chair and onto the floor. I lunge towards him, grabbing his beer bottle off the table and raising it above my head. Old timer turns and squints in panic – his attitude has gone, he's just an old drunk guy on the floor. And I'm a young man behaving like this is going to be a fair fight. I let the bottle slip out of my hand and it falls beside us.

This isn't who I want to be. I take a step away from him and look around the room. A whole bunch of strangers are staring at me like I'm some unhinged crazy person. The redhead is holding a phone up to her ear, no doubt calling the cops.

"Don't worry, I'm going," I say breathlessly, my adrenaline still pumping hard.

Sure, he deserved something, but I went way too far. It's like when the black mist comes, I have no control over myself. Now I'm walking out of the bar with another fucked up emotion I can't deal with, guilt.

Old timer keeps his eyes on me but doesn't move until I'm out the door. I gotta get out of this place. Not just this bar, but New York, Rhode Island, this whole damn area. I need a clean start.

By the time my next therapy session comes around I've already made up my mind.

"Dayton? I've never heard of it." My therapist scribbles down the name, no doubt to Google it later.

My cousin owns a ranch out there. I called him a couple of nights ago, after my ordeal with old timer. I don't call him often but when I do it's usually because I'm drunk or angry, usually both.

Tucker is older than me by eight years and since I lost my parents, he pretty much took that as a sign to occasionally try to father me despite living nine hundred miles away across the country. When he came to the funerals, he gave me a cell phone and said I could use it to call him anytime. I think he knew that as incredible as our grandmother was, it wasn't going to be easy. Grandma knew nothing about sports or what boys my age was into – it could be a lonely place to live.

My earliest memory of my dad was him setting up for football Sundays. We'd have chips and dip, cookies, sandwiches, Budweiser for him, Kool Aid for me; he'd sit with me and teach me all about the rules of the game whilst I watched on and thought about what a fucking awesome sport it was. I missed that the most when I lived with my grandma, her Sundays were usually church in the mornings and baking after. A far cry from what Dad gave me.

"Why Dayton?" she presses, distracting me from my memories.

"My cousin's there, it's a small town, for farming mostly, it's quiet and it looks absolutely nothing like New York. Which is the biggest appeal."

"Okay, well, as much as I think a fresh start could be a great opportunity, I'm not sure I can release you from therapy yet."

The memory of old timer lying on the floor and shielding himself from my fists springs to mind. She may have a point about the therapy thing but I'm not about to tell her that.

"I feel fine, I just know that I need to get away from this place. New York, Rhode Island… nothing but tough memories now."

Her eyebrow arches again, she's not buying my bullshit.

"Okay, how about we continue with therapy for another couple of months, but we'll do it by phone instead?"

I smile and agree to get her off my case and it seems to satisfy her. With nothing else holding me back, I load up the truck as soon as I'm home with the little belongings I have and head for Dayton, Tennessee.

Grandma's place is with the realtor and it's bound to sell quickly – the backyard overlooks an entire lake, it has a lot of land and it's been very well kept. For now, I still have inheritance from Mom and Dad, compensation from 9/11, thanks to George Bush, as well as all my savings from the Marines. That'll keep me going for a while.

CHAPTER FOUR

MADDISON

"Wow, this is actually really tasty."

He takes another mouthful of salmon and nods reassuringly at me.

"You sound surprised! I can whip up a decent meal in the kitchen now and then…" I playfully say, hoping to keep the mood light and positive.

He laughs a little before taking another bite.

"Sorry, I didn't mean to sound surprised. It's just really good."

"Thank you." I take a sip of my red wine feeling quite proud of myself. And Delia Smith of course, whose recipe this is.

"Keep eating foods like this and you'll lose that little extra weight in no time."

Cheers hun I think to myself as I down the rest of my red wine instead. Christ knows why it's so hard to pay me a simple compliment without following it up with some twat-of-the-year insult.

"I quite like how I look," I announce, testing the waters. I want to see what his reaction would be to someone actually being proud of their body and not feeling like they need to shed weight or aspire to having rock hard abs. After all, he is my boyfriend, surely he should find me attractive just as I am.

He drops his fork onto his plate with some irritation and stares up at me confused, as if he is trying to process what I said.

"Babe… come on, you don't have to lie to me."

"Jamie, I'm not lying. I'm honestly happy with how I look. I feel healthy."

Jamie presses the napkin against his lips, his eyes pondering what I've just said.

"Maddison, it's not just yourself you should be thinking of though. I have an entire brand to think of. I can't be seen with somebody who is happy to let themselves go; it doesn't align with my message."

Here's a message for you Jamie – why don't you go fuck yourself? Of course, I can't say that, I have to pick my battles and right now travelling with the girls is the one worth fighting for.

"You're right, maybe you can help me with a new workout regime."

I know full well by asking for his help that I'm massively massaging his ego which becomes obvious as he smiles and breathes a sigh of relief.

"Of course, babe, you'll need to go back to some strict calorie counting too."

It takes everything not to throw my fork at his head.

"Sounds great. We'll make a start when I'm back from my trip."

"Trip?" He locks eyes with me. *Oh shit, this is it, you've said it now Mads, don't back down.*

"Yes! Hannah and Poppy have invited me on this incredible trip to the States, it's like one giant excursion. We get picked up from the airport in Atlanta, then from there we travel to some amazing states before finishing in Florida. It's cheap too because we mostly stay in hostels…" I try to sound as upbeat as possible.

Jamie pushes his plate away like my trip idea has made him lose his appetite. I continue firing off the bullet points that I had mentally prepared in my head the night before.

"Before we get busier with the business and everything, I thought now would be the best time to let my hair down and travel a little with my best friends. It's totally safe too, we have a tour guide with us the entire time, and…"

"Safe? With them two slags? I'm hardly going to sleep well at night knowing Hannah of all people is leading you astray."

I try to hide my anger at that comment. I don't want this to end up in a huge row otherwise it'll be impossible for him to agree.

"Jamie… they're not slags. And even if they were I'm definitely not and you can trust me."

His middle finger rubs the side of his temple. I can sense he is getting wound up already and I haven't even told him how long it's for yet.

"So, backpacking around America?"

"Kind of, but we only visit five states so it's nothing too wild."

"How long for?"

Shit, here we go. What sounds better? Thirty-one days, four weeks or one month? I nervously tuck my hair behind my ears. Here we go.

"It's for the whole of June."

"A month!?" He snorts with a fake laugh like I'm insane.

"Yes…"

"And who will I get to replace you as my receptionist

for a month? Have you thought about anybody other than yourself?"

"Well, I spoke to this agency, and they can supply you with a receptionist for a month…"

"An agency?!"

He cuts me off before I have a chance to finish, slamming his hands down on the table angrily. It startles me and causes me to jump back in my seat.

"How can I be sure some random woman from an agency is going to be suitable? What if some overweight mess turns up?! Then what?"

The way he talks about women makes me feel sad. Like somehow being a little bigger makes you a terrible person.

He gets up from the table, pacing, rubbing the back of his head, growing more restless with me.

"And I just stay at home and work around the clock whilst you're off in some nightclub dressed like a cheap whore watching Hannah and Poppy jump from cock to cock."

That just shows how much he really knows my friends; Poppy is gay for starters and has been ever since she came out to me in a McDonald's when we were fourteen.

"What's your problem with my friends? They're not like that…"

"Oh come on, you see the way Hannah dresses."

"Yeah, she dresses like she's a confident woman with an insane body. She looks like a fucking Victoria's Secret model – if I looked like that, I'd probably dress the same!"

My voice has gone all high-pitched and defensive.

"She's not who I think you should be travelling with, that's all…"

"Well, I'm sorry, but none of the local Jehovah's Witnesses wanted to come away with me."

My sarcasm is the last straw. He stomps off to the bedroom, slamming the door behind him.

"I guess I'll clean up then," I mumble to myself, staring at all the plates and glasses.

I take the longest amount of time ever to wash the dishes, hoping that by the time I have finished, Jamie will be fast asleep and I can sneak into bed without any more arguing. I'm so frustrated that the two reasons he has to be so pissed off aren't real reasons at all. Insulting my friends and finding issue with a temporary receptionist he hasn't even met yet – he's impossible.

Once I've taken a good hour to clean the kitchen, I sit on the floor, pouring the last mouthful of red wine into my glass.

I think about my mum and her marriage to my dad. She adored him. She did everything to make him happy and let him make all the decisions, from where we went on holiday to which house we lived in, what car we bought, everything. And where did it leave her? Divorced.

If I'm not careful, I'm going to be just like Mum. I have to show Jamie that this is a relationship and not a dictatorship. I can make my own decisions. I want to go on this trip, I deserve to go and that's that.

I pull out my phone from my trouser pocket and start typing out a text before I can change my mind.

Han, please add one more to the booking. Pinging over my money now. USA here we come!!

Within seconds my phone pings back a message.

No fucking way? Jamie said yes?

He didn't. But I'll tell her that when we are on the plane.

CHAPTER FIVE

HENDRIX

I could get used to this. The silence out here is golden. The crickets chirping is all I can hear and all I can see for miles are fields and animals. Unless you head into the small local town you don't see many people, which is perfect for me because people quickly irritate me and nobody ever takes a shine to me anyway. I sound like an ass, but I don't trust people much – the last person I considered a friend turned out to be a rapist. I'm better off keeping myself to myself, I've had enough disappointment for one lifetime.

"I could really eat some of Aunty Kim's triple chocolate cookies right about now. Do you remember those Drix?"

I gulp hard on my beer. The mention of Mom's name always feels heavy and the sad truth is that I barely remember her face anymore, let alone things that she may have baked.

"I don't remember much anymore."

"Oh," Tucker looks guilty. "Well, she made the best cookies. I'm sure I have a copy of the recipe she used around here; I'll see if Savannah fancies the challenge."

Savannah is Tucker's wife. They're childhood sweethearts – they met in fifth grade when Savannah moved here from Alabama and became best friends; by sophomore year they were a lot more. They married in the little town's chapel as soon as they turned eighteen and that's that, they've been happily married ever since.

"So, what do you remember?" Tucker curiously asks.

"Bits and pieces. Football on Sundays with Dad, Mom hugging me goodbye at the school gates every morning. Never thought how soon it would be her last morning… Let's change the subject."

Tucker nods but clears his throat for another question.

"Sure. I have one question for you though…"

"If you're going to ask me what happened in the Marines, save your breath."

"But the Marines is all you've ever wanted to do. For you to get thrown out, something big must have happened…"

"It did, but that's all you need to know."

"Something happened with Martinez, didn't it?"

The name ruins my peaceful night and I know if I don't walk away now, I'll end up in a fight with my cousin and that's the last thing I want to do.

"I'm going to bed," I say instead.

Tucker immediately looks guilty.

"No, Hendrix, wait, I'm sorry. We can change the subject…"

I see on my watch that it's almost three in the morning now anyway. I'm tired after the long drive here and I don't have the patience to risk having the Marines brought up again. I need to walk away.

"It's all good, I'm just tired. Goodnight."

***

My head's a little heavy when I wake up on Tucker's couch. The humidity from the Tennessee heat is making me sweat already and it's barely ten in the morning. Last night was my first night here and Tucker sure wanted to make it memorable. We sat out on the porch drinking some home brew beer that tasted like ass really, but God it was strong. Of course, I didn't tell Tucker that, he thinks I loved it. As much as it was decent of Tucker to offer me to stay with him for as long as I need, last night's conversation gave me a kick up the ass to get sorted. I can't stay here and be smothered by questions that I'll never want to answer, and I need my own space.

When I get into town and see it properly in the daylight, it's even smaller than I thought but pretty much everything you need is here on one strip of road. Either side of the road is a string of shops, barbers, butchers, a coffee place, supermarket and bakery and a doctors' office. Thankfully, there's one realtor too which I head to first.

My budget is decent but that doesn't mean I want some white picket fence family home for me to rattle around in. I couldn't think of anything sadder.

Through the glass of Real Estate Creek, my eyes fixate on a picture of a cabin. It looks small enough for one guy but has a decent amount of land, which is exactly what I need – space. The cabin has a veranda wrapped around it, two American flags proudly hanging high up from the wood, and a large gravel driveway for my truck; tall trees surround the property and, right at the back, there's a creek. But the bonus is, no neighbours.

In the corner of my eye through the glass, I see the realtor undoing another button on her white blouse, showing off her fake tits. She would put Dolly Parton to shame with those.

"Looking for a bachelor pad?" She confidently appears in the doorway of the store, one arm above her head, leaning against the frame, shoulders back, pushing her cleavage in my face. She has to be mid-forties, short blonde hair made as big as possible with at least four cans of hairspray no doubt.

"I'm looking for somewhere I can be alone, ma'am, that's all."

"Come inside, let's see what deal we can do for you."

I keep my answers short and minimal as she fires question after question at me, telling me how she's never seen me around town before and asking where I've come from, what made me move here; of course, her eyes brighten the more she confirms for herself that I'm not tied down to a relationship. I try to keep to the topic of the cabin only.

"Well, the property is available straight away. The last owners moved down to Florida and they wanted a quick sale, hence the price."

She gets up from her desk, heads straight to the door and flips over the sign that changes it from open to closed.

"Of course, with how keen they are to sell, I could probably get a much better deal for you."

I struggle to conceal my sigh, knowing exactly where this is going, but my response doesn't faze her at all. She stands between my legs and leans back onto her desk slightly, allowing her skirt to hitch up, showing off the lace part of her black stockings.

I lean back in my chair, deciding whether I want to fuck her or not. It would be easy to, she's offering it on a plate, but my last fuck with some blonde in the bar parking lot back home was a disaster. Apparently not taking her phone number or promising to see her again made me a jerk.

Big hair pulls at my belt buckle and straddles me and before I know it, I'm inside her, making her moan and tremble. I, however, am not even close. In fact, it's a relief that she finishes quickly, and it seems easier to pretend that I did too.

"My name is Maggie, by the way," she tells me, like I care, as she buttons her blouse back up and looks at me with satisfaction.

The only thing I'm satisfied with is that the cabin is now mine, and ten percent cheaper too.

She scribbles down her personal phone number on some scrap paper and tells me she'll come over to help me get settled. I throw the piece of paper Maggie or Mollie gave me straight into the trash the second I'm outside, I have zero interest entertaining that again.

The keys to my new cabin will be ready for me by the end of next week, but I do a little drive by to see it by myself first. I quickly realise it's only a five-minute drive down the road from the ranch which works out well since Tucker says he has work for me down there. It's so secluded that it suits me perfectly.

CHAPTER SIX

MADDISON

Jamie made it known he was still in a bad mood with me this morning when he huffed and sighed and slammed kitchen cupboard doors behind him. I lay in bed with my eyes closed, pretending that I was miraculously sleeping through it. It's Saturday morning and Jamie usually goes out at the crack of dawn to do his own workouts and then, when he is home, we plan something to do and spend the rest of the day together. But this morning, he sent me a very blunt text message which said he has a meeting at lunchtime and then he is off for an early dinner at his mum's house. My lack of invite is my punishment for wanting to go travelling.

I can't let it deter me though; at some point he'll have to suck it up because the more I think about it, the more I know this trip is for me. I need it.

I was thinking a lot about my mum and dad last night and something dawned on me. I thought I was being careful not to be like Mum and put a man first but that's exactly what I have done. The fact that I've become such a people pleaser depressed me. I was in my first year of veterinary school, studying hard for my dream career, when I met Jamie. He pleaded with me to take a year out of my studies so that I could support him in getting his business off the ground but all I am is his glorified personal assistant with absolutely no end in sight. Christ, he doesn't even want me to take a month out for travel – he's hardly going to be happy when I say I want to go back to university and finish my degree.

Then of course I had to move in with him. At the time I put his actions down as romantic and thoughtful but now I feel like it was just so that he could get his own damn way as usual. I was flat sharing with Hannah and Poppy; between the three of us our rent was small, and the apartment was pretty. We had a balcony overlooking the city, right in the thick of all the action; it was great fun – we'd often reference ourselves as the real Carrie, Samantha and Charlotte from *Sex and the City*.

But then Jamie felt that Hannah was being irresponsible bringing home different men and that I'd end up in some Netflix documentary as a victim of a psychopathic serial killer. In the end he even phoned my own mum and completely exaggerated Hannah's rendezvous to the point he worried her sick and, before I knew it, she was phoning me most days pleading with me to move in with Jamie, where, in her words, "it's safer and you can concentrate on your own life more".

So I did. Somehow, within a matter of months, I was living with Jamie, and I had put my studies on hold to support him. I was already becoming just like my mum, putting a man before myself and letting go of my own ambitions to appease everybody else.

Isn't it funny how you can believe you're happy and completely in love one minute and the next it's like a switch has gone off and you see the relationship in a whole different light?

I push thoughts of Jamie to the back of my mind and take myself off shopping. I debate for half an hour about a pair of black cowboy boots with a cute brown pattern stitched on them. I go back and forth on whether I can pull them off. What would Jamie say? Besides ridiculing me. The staff are side-eyeing me, no doubt worried I'm going to try and steal them or something, I am taking such a weirdly long time to make up my mind. Eventually, I decide to buy the boots. Where else can you wear cowboy boots if not in a state like Tennessee, so well-known for its country music? Plus, it suits my new attitude – the *just fucking do it* attitude. Okay, it's hardly a philosophical Buddha-style quote but it's working for me.

I hit more shops, buying cute little white tops that I can easily throw together with some denim shorts or floaty skirts, just things that are quick and easy but comfortable to wear. If I'm going to be living out of a suitcase, I need to make it all as simple as possible. I buy beach waves hair mousse too and think what a genius I am – I can use this on my rushed, messy hair days and make it look like I'm doing it on purpose. I buy a couple more bra sets, bikinis, a few dresses in case we go somewhere a little dressier in the evenings and I choose a comfortable pair of white trainers. A few new pieces of make-up and six bottles of mosquito repellent later and I feel ready.

Although this whole day has already given me a massive boost, I realise I don't want to stop here. I decide I deserve a pamper too and swing by the beauty salon on my way home. I get some ashy blonde highlights put through my chocolate brown hair and get my nails freshly painted with a little pedicure to match. I've gone for subtle white tips which I think look really classy. I practically skip home when I'm finished – this trip can't come quickly enough. Just six more days to go.

I have all my new clothes out on the bed when I hear Jamie come through the front door. I was going to try everything on but suddenly that urge has passed.

"How was it at your mum's?" I speak first, nervous because he is already eyeing up my clothes in confusion.

"Yeah, it was fine. She wrapped up some quiche and bits for you, I left it in the kitchen."

"Oh lovely. I'll text her and thank her shortly."

"What's all this?" he asks irritably.

Here we go.

"I went shopping today, I wanted to get myself organised for my trip and I was in desperate need of more shorts and comfortable trainers."

"So what are these?" He picks up one of the cowboy boots, smirking in a mocking way that instantly makes me feel embarrassed.

"Well, you know, I've always loved them and if you can't pull them off in Tennessee where can you, right?"

"For some girls maybe, but you can't pull these off Mads. Have you even checked if they fit over your calves?"

"Yes! I have, thank you." I snatch the boot out of his hands, feeling my defensive barrier going up. Is he implying my legs are too fat for boots? His opinion of me is really starting to grate, especially since I'm average sized. I'm not fat in the slightest. Just because I don't have rock hard abs doesn't mean there's something wrong with me.

"Maddie, this is ridiculous. I don't know why you've wasted money on all these clothes. We both know you're not going."

"I am going Jamie," I confirm with as much confidence as possible.

"Come on, this isn't you, you're not the adventurous type, you're going to hate it."

Not as much as I'm beginning to hate my life with him.

"I don't know that though. I need to do this. I feel like since I left my course for you, I've lost myself and…"

"So it's my fault?" He cuts me off rashly, his arms crossed, looking ready for an argument that I don't want.

"I'm just saying, I feel a bit lost."

He paces the room, his hand rubbing the back of his head again. I know only too well that this means he is losing his patience with me.

"You know what you are, Maddison?"

His face is red with anger.

"You are so unbelievably self-centred. I give you a decent place to live, I give you a job, I help you stay in shape, I *fucking* do everything!"

"But I didn't ask you to! I don't know why or how it's got like this, but I don't want that. I feel like a housewife from the forties. I feel like what I want doesn't matter."

He steps closer to me, his eyes fixed on mine; his demeanour frightens me, the look in his eyes is a look I've never seen before, it's unkind and cold.

"We don't have sex enough, do we? That's what you want isn't it? Because that's what girls who go travelling want don't they? One-night stands with strange men. I can fuck you like that if that's what you need..."

He pulls at his belt buckle, immediately undoing his top trouser button.

"What? Don't be ridiculous Jamie! That's insane. That's not it at all."

My voice is strained as I try to conceal my fear but with no luck. Something about this trip has pushed a button in him I didn't know he had, he looks at me with hatred.

"Come on Maddie, get naked. Hell, I'll fuck you in your boots if that's what it takes. That's what you want right? Fucked in your whore boots? Like a slut?"

Tears sting my eyes before spilling down my cheeks. I hadn't even realised I was getting so emotional.

He grabs my arm and pushes my hand against the bulge

through his boxers.

"Fuck you!" I scream before pushing him away.

"No, fuck you Maddison, you're the one making me like this!"

I grab my phone and get the hell out of the apartment as quickly as I can. I'm halfway down the street before I realise I didn't put any shoes on. I'm barefoot in the light summer evening, mascara-stained tears down my face, my heart beating out of my chest. I look a sight for sore eyes and probably a little like a homeless person too.

What the fuck just happened?

CHAPTER SEVEN

HENDRIX

Tucker is impressed at how quickly I sorted a place to live when I tell him that evening, even more impressed with how close it is to the ranch.

Savannah makes us burgers for dinner before suggesting we all go down to the bar to toast my new home. The bar is named the Old Creek Saloon and it's as old yet charming as everything else in this town. I still love how worlds apart from the east coast it is.

One foot inside the bar and everybody is quick to stare, which so far is the only negative of moving here. You'd think I was a Martian and not just a New Yorker.

"Don't worry, it's because you're new. They'll get used to it after a while," Tucker says with a grin; he finds it amusing watching me trying to keep my cool under the spotlight of a bunch of nosey rednecks.

Everyone has been nice enough I suppose, but they all treat me like a shiny new toy.

"I'll have a whiskey, thanks." I order my drink and take my seat next to Tucker who orders the same.

Savannah orders an iced tea.

"Come on, it's the weekend, you don't want something stronger? I thought we were celebrating!" I say, turning to the bartender. "Get the lady a glass of house white please." She locks eyes with Tuck straight away and they giggle and whisper something about a secret.

They nod at each other, and Tuck gives her a gentle kiss against her temple before turning back to me.

"We're pregnant!" they announce cheerily.

Tucker has this huge beaming smiling on his face, full of pride and happiness.

"Fuck! That's fucking awesome!"

I lean across and kiss Savannah on the cheek. I know this must mean a lot to them. Tucker doesn't talk about it much, but I know they have had difficulties; last I heard was when I was deployed, and Grandma told me Savannah had suffered a third miscarriage.

"Thank you! I knew eventually God would answer my prayers." I'm definitely not religious, but I admire that Savannah has always kept her faith no matter what and I guess it's great that she finds comfort from it. Even if it sounds like a lot of BS to me.

"Well done man!" I tell Tuck as we chink our whiskey glasses together.

The next half hour, Savannah chews my ear off with nursery ideas and baby names and God knows what else. If she were anybody else, I'd have got up and left already, but she's a good woman. I like her a lot and after their losses, even I can appreciate how much she deserves to share her excitement. Even if I am bored shitless.

I'm four whiskeys in, listening to Tucker tell me about his plan to buy a lot of wood and make everything for the nursery himself when a man I don't know grabs me by my shoulder and pulls me round in my chair.

"You! You're the motherfucker who slept with my wife!"

I laugh, poor guy must be confused. I push his hand off my shoulder, not really fazed by the scene he is making in the busy bar.

"Married women aren't my style sir; you must be mistaken."

"So you didn't have sex with Maggie today? In her office?"

"Oh," the penny drops, "that woman? Yeah, I fucked her," I answer before turning back around in my chair and taking a mouthful of whiskey.

I notice Tucker's jaw has dropped open.

"What?" I shrug. "I didn't know she was married."

"You son of a bitch!" the man yells from behind me and shoves me hard against the bar.

"Pete, come on, he didn't know, you don't want to fight him, okay. He's sorry." Tucker puts his hands out defensively.

"I'm not sorry..."

"Yes, you are..."

"I've done nothing wrong. His wife offered herself to me on a plate, that's not my fault."

Pete attempts to grab me by my t-shirt but Tucker holds him back.

"You don't want to do this Pete, he's ex-Marine okay, he's had it rough lately, come on, just walk away."

"Yeah Pete, just walk away," I tease as I raise my whiskey to my lips again.

This guy who I've never seen before but who I now know is called Pete begins to walk away and I should really leave it at that, but I can't help myself.

"She wasn't very good anyway."

And with that, Pete swings back around but before his fist can connect with my face, I grab his hand and twist it so far around his back I can feel it ready to snap. As Pete winces in pain, I head butt him hard between the eyes. He drops to the floor, cradling his bloody nose and groaning in agony.

"What?" I ask the audience of gawping onlookers.

Their expressions look angry – if this were a hundred years ago, they'd be chasing me out of here with pitchforks right now, I'm sure.

"Tucker!" the angry bartender shouts from across the room, like Tucker is my father and he needs to get me in line.

"We're leaving," he assures the man, and he pushes me impatiently off my stool and out the door.

The second we head into the street and I feel the fresh albeit humid air, I realise the whiskeys have hit me harder than I thought.

"Is whiskey stronger out here?"

But Tuck is in no mood for my joking.

"Seriously, you've been here twenty-four hours and you slept with a married woman?"

"I swear, I didn't know she was married, I didn't even know her name until after."

I glance at Savannah, and I must admit, her sad face is the only thing that brings me a sense of guilt.

"He's a good man is Pete, and you're right, it's not your fault, it's Maggie and her promiscuous ways. But you didn't have to hurt him Hendrix, he didn't deserve that." If I'm not mistaken her eyes have tears in them.

She stares at me momentarily like she wants to say more but instead turns on her heel and walks up the dusty road back towards the ranch.

She disappears quickly into the night and before I have a chance to apologise, Tucker chases after her, leaving me behind to make my own way back. The fact I'm on my own now speaks volumes as to how pissed they are at me.

The thought of upsetting them sobers me – they're the only family I have left, and I've already disappointed them, but they don't know I'm angry all the fucking time and concealing it isn't easy. Especially when some man comes up to me all guns blazing. But then I feel myself getting angry *for* being angry *all* the time. It's so fucked up, it's part of a vicious cycle that I have been stuck in now for as long as I can remember. Between losing my folks and seeing Martinez do the unthinkable, the world is so fucking ugly and I'm tired of it.

As luck would have it, there's one liquor store still open in town and since I'm everybody's least favourite person right now, I think I'll get myself a bottle of Jack and sit alone by the creek, out of everyone's way.

CHAPTER EIGHT

MADDISON

I haven't seen or spoken to Jamie in three days which I didn't think would be possible seeing as I work for him in reception, but he has kept his distance from the branch I'm in and seems to be hovering around the others instead. I told Hannah and Poppy about the argument, well some of it, I had to really since I'm now crashing on their sofa. I didn't say Jamie tried to have sex with me or even half of the names he called me in the process, I just said that he is majorly offended by me wanting to go on this trip and he feels like I'm ungrateful for everything he has done. Hannah rolled her eyes whilst I offloaded the whole thing onto them. I sense she knew that there was more to the argument, but she didn't push me to reveal more than I was comfortable with.

Poppy was incredibly kind and gentle as always; she tried to defend me whilst being careful not to condemn Jamie in the process. I thought it was really classy of her to be fair, she'd make a great therapist one day. However, Poppy is also a huge feminist and if she knew that he tried to push me into having sex with him, she'd likely have a whole different view.

I'm halfway through my second cup of coffee of the morning when a huge bouquet of yellow roses is placed on my desk by a cheery looking woman wearing a 'Next day Bouquet' t-shirt which is actually a pretty catchy slogan for a flower delivery company.

"Wow!" They're impressive for sure, beautifully hand-picked yellow roses tied together with little white gypsophila, all arranged very aesthetically with a yellow ribbon tying them together and placed in an ivory-coloured box.

"Maddison Mulligan?"

"Oh! Yes, that's me." Uh oh, this must mean they're guilt flowers from Jamie.

"Great! Sign here please." I lazily scribble my name down on her clipboard, not really sure if I even want to accept them but it doesn't feel fair to her to refuse them, she's just doing her job. She gives a satisfied nod and disappears out of the office. I glance at the little ivory envelope, no doubt there's an apology inside. The saddest thing is that I'm not sure there is anything that Jamie can say to make me feel any better.

Meet me at home tonight, 7pm – J.

Of course, I should have known he'd want to apologise on his terms. I suppose everyone deserves a chance to say sorry. God, I don't know how to feel. I've slumped back down in my chair, staring at the flowers that somehow aren't as beautiful as I thought they were moments ago. The people pleaser in me is somehow feeling sorry for *him.* Like poor Jamie must be feeling so guilty and going out of his mind with worry, he must feel sick over how he made me feel. Then there's this little voice inside, the voice that keeps pushing my *just fucking do it* attitude, and it's giving me ideas to just avoid him until I'm on that plane, then I can have the best time away and worry about it when I'm home. And to be fair, a month's worth of cold shoulder is the least he deserves.

***

"Just don't let him make you feel bad, Mads. You deserve this, remember?"

"I know Han, don't worry, I've got this." I'm on a three-way Facetime with the girls as I kill time in a cocktail bar near work called The Tipsy Tiger. It's this whole jungle themed bar with huge colourful cocktails, extremely Instagrammable of course, and it's two for one for the next hour so I'm making the most of it. I have wanted to come here for a while, but Jamie would start lecturing me on the number of sugars in these cocktails and it just didn't seem worth the headache. Although I wish now that I just did what *I* wanted, because this Pink Flamingo is insanely delicious and refreshing.

"We are here anytime you need us; you know that right?"

"Thank you Pops, I love you girls. I'll text you later."

I keep an eye on the time, five forty-five, six o'clock, six fifteen… The closer it gets to seven, the more I dread seeing him. I'm not scared of him as such, but the other night was a shock, it's almost like he had a pure hatred for me. How can you tell somebody you love them but then want to hurt them so much? It doesn't make any sense; our relationship doesn't make sense anymore.

It's still two for one on the cocktails so it'd be rude not to order another. This time I order two Rainforest Revenge drinks, which almost blow my head off in one sip. It has pineapple juice, grenadine, rum, vodka, orange gin, tequila and triple sec. A few more sips and my head is feeling a lot lighter, but it's not until I stagger to the toilet that I realise that I'm half cut. I catch myself in the bathroom mirror. I look kind of hot. The extra pounds that Jamie is so concerned about actually highlight the curves on my hips and give me a little extra booty. My skin is the best I have seen it in a long time and my make-up is light and dewy, making me look refreshed. My new nude lipstick is subtle but makes my lips fuller; both my eyes and lips are really standing out.

"Well, I'd bang you just as you are…" I tell my reflection. "Fuck Jamie! You're literally a bad bitch. We might even listen to some Cardi B on the way home, because why not?"

I'm full on attempting to twerk as I sing WAP to myself. I have no idea if it's the rum, but my confidence is sky high right now.

"Okay, listen up Maddie, you sexy bitch. You're a strong ass woman, you got this! Any shit from Jamie the giant prick and… Hang on, that's like James and the giant peach. I'm so good at these insults, I should save them up and tell them to him later."

My words are slurring but, in my head, I am extremely articulate and confident in my ability to stand up to Jamie. I head back to the bar, down the rest of my cocktail and order an Uber. I need to see Jamie now whilst I'm feeling this feisty.

I barely make it to the third floor of the building where Jamie is already waiting at the front door of the apartment for me.

"That's spooky! You a psychic now?"

"No, I just heard what sounded like somebody falling up some stairs followed by a tonne of abuse at the craftmanship of said stairwell. I'm surprised that it's you though."

"Of course you're surprised it's me – it's not at all refined and how a girlfriend of Jamie's should be behaving is it?"

I push past him and collapse onto the sofa, kicking my heels off.

"Did you get the flowers?" Jamie asks, calmly closing the door behind us.

"Yes, I did and I'm not sure I accept the apology."

I sit with my arms folded, ready for him to grovel.

"I didn't apologise."

"But… that was the intention behind them, wasn't it?"

"Not really. It was more of an olive branch for you. If anyone should be apologising, it's you Maddison."

I throw my arms in the air like a crazy person. I can't fathom how he has come to this conclusion.

"How do you work that out?"

"Maddison, baby, you were being totally unreasonable. We didn't even discuss this trip; you just decided all on your own."

I let out a huge, disappointed sigh.

"That's just it, Jamie, I feel like I have to ask for permission for anything I want to do and that's not your fault, it's me. I have put your needs above my own, I put my own career on hold to support yours, I have danced to the beat of your drum throughout our entire relationship. And now here we are. I have totally lost who I am, and you're so used to me being more of a PA than a girlfriend that you forget I have my own dreams and ambitions too."

"But…"

"No Jamie, just listen to me please because God knows if I don't say it now, I'm not sure when I will. You totally crossed the line the other night, whipping off your belt like that, throwing your weight around, demanding sex. What message does that give? I have dealt with your comments about my weight, and I have put up with your misogynistic comments towards my friends and women in general, but I'm not going to let you scare me like that ever again!"

"I didn't mean to scare you, I was frustrated." He answers so quickly that I'm a little annoyed he didn't take at least a second to absorb what I have said.

"Well, it doesn't make it right."

"You're right. It doesn't and that's why I have a solution. I'm coming with you – not for the whole time because I can't leave the business that long, but I'll be there for the first two weeks and then for the last two weeks you can Facetime me three times a day…"

The thought of Jamie coming with me makes the entire trip lose its charm.

"Well? Say thank you then."

I pause in thought, staring anxiously down at the floor. Only Jamie could believe that a solution would be him chauffeuring me on this trip like I'm a child.

"No, no I can't Jamie. That isn't a solution, that's you still trying to control something that I want to do. I can't do this anymore."

Tears stream down my face which is only a tiny reflection of how I'm feeling inside. I'm bubbling up like an active volcano. He *isn't* listening. He *never* listens. I could shout what I want from the rooftops, and he wouldn't get it. This relationship has gone from chipping away at me to fully tearing me down. It *has* to stop, it *has* to.

I stand up, pacing back and forth, and just as Jamie reaches out to console me, I snap, and the words fall out.

"It's over Jamie, I'm sorry, I can't be with you anymore."

CHAPTER NINE

HENDRIX

I wake up to the sound of a mug of coffee being placed gently down on the porch next to my head. The cold hard wood against my cheek reminds me of how drunk I got myself last night; it doesn't take long to realise I passed out here at some point in the early hours.

My eyelids flicker open just quickly enough to see who left the mug of coffee; I catch a glimpse of Savannah heading back into the house. Even though she's pissed at me, she still remains one of the most considerate people I have ever met and that only adds to the guilt I was trying to drink away last night.

"Get your shit together Hendrix, I need your help." Tucker rushes his words as he walks straight past me and towards the pickup truck. My head spins the second I sit up, but Tuck's urgency makes me push through it. He barely makes eye contact when I pull myself into the worn-out seat next to him. His creamy coloured cowboy hat is low today; I guess he is trying to hide his frown.

I never understood his obsession with cowboy hats but then again, I'm a city boy, so I guess I wouldn't.

"What's going on?"

"Three of the horses got out last night, one of them pregnant, and Savannah is worried sick that she's gonna get hit by one of the truckers on the main road. I need your help to lead them back."

His tone is flat. I can't really read him, but I think I can assume that my bar fight last night has majorly disappointed him.

We travel in silence, apart from the low volume of the local radio playing through the speakers. Tucker pulls over a couple of times to look at the map and see which other routes the horses could have taken; we've been driving around for twenty or so minutes so far and not spotted one of them.

"How pregnant is she?" is my best attempt at having a neutral conversation.

"Savannah or the horse?"

"Oh, I meant the horse."

He smirks. "I know you did." I'm relieved for the momentary break in his frown. "I don't know to be honest; we haven't gotten around to getting the vet out, but she's definitely getting big now."

"What did ya'll name her?"

"Ya'll? Is the way we talk rubbing off on you already?"

Never in my life have I said ya'll. I've barely been here a week.

"I always thought it was annoying how you spoke when we grew up, but I guess it is seriously contagious!"

I'm happy when Tuck smiles again, I feel like I'm somehow lifting his mood and making up for last night.

"Savannah named her Moonlight."

"Cool," I respond, running out of things to say, but thankfully Tucker's phone rings and breaks the short silence.

"Hello? Oh my god, baby, that's incredible news! Alright, we're heading back."

"They're found?"

"Yeah! Savannah said she was feeding the chickens and out of nowhere all three of them appeared. They found their way back."

"Wow!"

"Yeah, wow. Damn horses nearly gave me a heart attack."

We spin around and head back to the ranch. I suddenly catch my reflection – slight stubble coming through, dark circles around my eyes, looking like I've been binge-drinking for days.

My hair is still the same buzz cut I've had since I first enrolled in the Marines. Although it's the same colour as Tucker's, his style is very different, his brown hair is reaching his shoulders and he has had it that way since we were kids.

I stare at the tattoo that covers the entirety of my throat; it was the last tattoo I got, and I had it done weeks after being kicked out of the Marines, since tattoos were forbidden on the neck. It's an American Eagle, the head covers my Adam's apple with the wings spreading across my neck. It means power and strength, at least that's what my dad told me when I was a kid.

Most of my tattoos mean something in one way or another. Across my left ribcage I have a dark blue butterfly; I only got this because it's a copy of the one small tattoo my mom had. It was tiny and she had it done on her wrist, but she loved it; she said it was a spur of the moment thing on the honeymoon with my dad, she said life is about spontaneous moments like that. No thinking, no pre-planning, just go for it.

"Look Hendrix, I gotta talk to you about last night."

Tucker's voice snaps me out of my daydream. Shit, I'm no good at confrontation, I just get angry, and I hate that side of me.

"Savannah was in tears last night. She was heartbroken for Pete…"

"He started on me!" I deflect.

"Well yeah. But with good reason, you did fuck his wife."

I shake my head irritably but choose not to try and defend it.

"Thing is, Pete has been through a lot. About four years ago he was diagnosed with lung cancer. He was doing well, the treatments were working, and he was having a lot of good days, but in the last year the good days got less and less. His wife got bored of him being ill all the time and it's a well-known fact she goes about town entertaining anyone who gives her a second look."

Well don't I feel like an ass.

"He is a very unwell man who should be taking it easy and being looked after, but I guess that's not easy when your wife is out making a mockery of your marriage vows. God,

Savannah hates her so much – it's the only time I have ever heard her use the C-word."

"Woah!"

"Yeah, exactly. She's protective of Pete, the whole town is, you can understand why."

I ponder the information for a moment.

"No wonder everyone hates me."

Tucker sighs whilst rearranging his cowboy hat.

"People will realise soon enough that you didn't know Pete was ill or that Maggie was married. You're not the first guy Pete has gotten into it with and sadly, you probably won't be the last."

"Maybe I should talk to Pete next time I see him, perhaps I could clear the air."

"Or maybe you could just stop losing your temper and upsetting everybody."

The tone behind his words catches me completely off guard – he makes it sound like I'm a problem when he is the one who has always told me to move here. I may lose my temper but, on this occasion, I hardly think I should be expected to take the full blame.

"I get it Tuck," I snap.

"I don't know if you do though. It's different around here, a small working town like this is nothing like the east coast. We look after each other here, we become like family. You can't just go throwing your weight around."

"Oh, fuck's sake, Tucker, really?"

"Really!" he snaps back. "You've had this same attitude forever. I thought when you went into the Marines you'd grow out if it, but if anything, you've come out worse."

"So sorry Tuck, I had no idea you felt that way, but when you were out here playing farmer boy some of us were dealing with the ugly side of the world!" I grit my teeth to stop me saying anymore; my body is already tensing as the anger takes a hold of me.

"Oh, because you're the only person who has been through hardship, right?"

"I'm the only one in the family getting my ass shot at to protect this country, yeah."

"Congratulations Hendrix, but you practically ran to the Marines because you were running away from home."

"Fuck you! You know nothing. Pull over the damn car."

"No, we're going back to the ranch, we got work to do."

Without thinking I punch the dashboard in front of me.

"Dammit Tuck, pull over the fucking car now!"

My voice is loud and threatening and I flash Tucker a warning glare. He doesn't hesitate, he grinds the truck to a halt, and I jump out quickly, slamming the door hard behind me.

CHAPTER TEN

MADDISON

After twenty-plus airport selfies, Hannah, Poppy and I are finally boarding the jumbo jet to Atlanta. I have never been to Atlanta before, well actually, I've never been to the States before, apart from when I was four and we all went to Orlando, but of course I have no memory of that, so everything feels brand new.

My phone pings for the seventh time since we got to the airport. I glance down but already know it'll be Jamie again.

> *If you get on that plane, you're fired. Call*
> *me asap to sort this out!*

"Jamie again?" Hannah asks as she peers over my shoulder to look at my phone.

"Yep, but he has given up being nice."

In the past three hours I have had messages from him telling me he loves me, messages saying that he doesn't want to break up, messages saying he'll wait for me and now this. Threatening to fire me from a job I can't stand and only took in the first place to help him out. This isn't a threat, it's a bloody blessing.

I turn my phone off – eight hours without contact from Jamie will be heaven. He didn't take the break-up well, he accused me of all sorts, from affairs to having a mid-life crisis. I laughed at the mid-life crisis suggestion, only a truly arrogant guy like Jamie could assume the only reason why a woman would want to break up with him would be due to a breakdown. I push Jamie to the back of my mind. I don't want to let him stress me out or take up my thoughts, this is a once in a lifetime trip and I intend on making the most of it.

I relax into my seat, stick my headphones in my ears and click shuffle on my playlist titled *Plane Songs* – yes, I'm that person. In front of me is a small tv screen which shows the map of our journey. I love so much how far away I'll be. I really feel like for the first time in a long while, I can have the space to think for myself and be who I want to be. Within an hour Hannah is onto her third prosecco and Poppy is fast asleep with her head resting on my shoulder; her short blonde spikey hair keeps tickling my face which prompts Hannah to tease me for it. I've laughed more on this plane journey already than I had in the last few months. That fact comforts me – you know when you just feel like you need reassurance that you made the right decision on something, well I definitely just had it.

As soon as we land in Atlanta, we find our tour guide who is holding up a sign in front of a coach. It's exciting seeing different people arrive from different areas of the world but all coming together for this trip. Hannah instantly takes a shine to someone called Luiz, a young Brazilian guy; he is very 'Abercrombie & Fitch' attractive and I'm certain he is used to female attention, but even so, he still looks slightly scared by Hannah's advances which has me and Poppy in hysterics.

By the time the coach pulls into the hostel car park, or parking lot now that we are state side, a lot of us have had time to get acquainted and it's exciting to see that everyone is friendly and totally up for fun. There's such a mix of us and it's really liberating to meet so many people. We aren't the only English travellers, there's a few from up North and one Scottish girl, and there's also Australians, Spanish, South Africans and French to name a few.

"I had no idea there'd be so many different people."

"Pretty cool huh – and to think you nearly didn't come!" Hannah playfully nudges me, but she is right. On what planet would I turn this down for… Actually, never mind, we aren't thinking about him right now.

The humidity in Atlanta is unforgiving; my white t-shirt is already damp and sticking to me uncomfortably. The tour guide tells us to get some rest as we'll start exploring the city bright and early but of course nobody pays too much attention to that, we are all far too excited. It's early evening here and my stomach is growling with hunger. Hannah noticed a fried chicken vendor on our drive in, so we decide to head there and oh my god, she picked well. The piece of chicken is huge and succulent and seasoned to perfection, and the small fries I ordered are actually big enough to feed a family of four, but I don't complain – after eight hours of pretzels and unappealing plane food, this is heaven.

Just as I bite into some more chicken, a disapproving stare from Jamie flashes into my mind. He's just stood there, staring at my body and then back at the greasy chicken, judging me.

"What's wrong?" Hannah asks as I drop my chicken back down into my paper plate.

"I don't know, one second I was enjoying it and the next I felt... guilty..."

"Let me guess, Jamie wouldn't want you eating this, right? After all, you're dating the face of *the private members health club!*" she jeers, making Poppy giggle. "And you must eat rice and vegetables with salad and no dressing, you must be a size zero, drink water only and somehow be happy about it too! Bore off Jamie!"

I'm mad at myself for somehow allowing Jamie to enter my mind and dampen my day. He is thousands of miles away and yet I can feel him looking down his nose on me.

"You okay? We were just kidding." Poppy reaches out and comforts me by stroking my arm.

I pause for a moment, not really sure if I am, but I'm adamant I will be.

"Yeah, I'll be fine, it's just frustrating. I keep telling myself not to think of him."

"Well that's fucking stupid," Poppy laughs. "Think about it, if I told you not to think about a pink elephant, what are you thinking about?"

Straight away, I'm somehow thinking about a huge pink elephant standing on the street in Atlanta.

"A pink elephant..."

"Exactly! You can't tell your mind not to do something, it doesn't work that way. It'll just take time you know. When you've been with someone for so long who dictates everything you do, your mind is bound to worry about what he'll say. Eventually, you'll do more and more, and you won't even worry about him. The coolest thing is that you won't even realise your brain is healing, it'll just happen and one day you'll realise it's been weeks and you've not stressed over him once."

I love Poppy's advice; she seriously needs to complete her counselling degree already. She's going to be a real asset to a lot of people who need the voice of reason.

"Yeah, so come on, get that greasy chicken in your stomach girl! Because according to Google Maps we are only five minutes away from a cake shop, so that's dessert sorted!" Hannah whips her long blonde hair back off her shoulders in a way that would make Beyonce truly proud. Between her sassiness and Poppy's comforting words, I really feel like I'm going to be okay. Like Poppy said, it'll take time, but I'll get there.

CHAPTER ELEVEN

HENDRIX

I end up in the same bar I brawled in last night. I half expect to be barred but instead the owner makes a comment about me being Tucker's cousin and so he is willing to let it slide this once but one foot out of line and I'll be banned for life. If it were back home, I'd probably laugh in his face and walk out; there's hundreds of bars back home, I wouldn't put up with being spoken to like a naughty kid, but since this is the only bar for miles, I grin and bear it.

The bar is dead during the day, it's just me and one other guy who is sat at the other end of the bar. I don't mind though, it's better than being around people, I just let them down anyway. I'm taking a sip of my third whiskey when I hear the faint cries of a woman; it's hard to make out what she's saying but the sound is blood-curdling – it's enough to know something awful has happened.

The barman drops his towel along with the pint glass he was polishing and runs straight to the window.

"Holy shit! It's the school, it's up in flames!"

I spin round in my chair and, out of the window, I see thick black smoke rising up to the sky.

Fuck, it's bad. As soon as I'm outside I see how much of the building is already engulfed in flames – it's spreading quickly. I make my way down the street to the gates and see nothing but a bunch of crying parents and screaming kids fleeing. There are no firefighters in sight.

"Where's the fire truck?" I call back to the barman who is frantically ushering the kids away from the building and towards the bar.

I can barely hear him through the chaos.

"One fire department here covers four towns. They could be a while!" he calls before turning back towards the bar.

"My kid is still in there!" a woman screams. She's collapsed on the sidewalk; her white long-sleeved t-shirt has rips and soot all over it and a cut on her head suggests she has tried getting into the building already. Tears stream down her flushed cheeks and she looks shaken in fear.

"Ma'am, what is your child's name?" I bend down to her level, trying to get her to focus on me and not the inferno in front of us.

"Casey, her name is Casey and she's six years old. Oh God." She throws her head back as terror sets in. "Not my Casey, God, please no!" She lets out an agonised scream and clutches her chest.

I look around; still no sign of a fire truck, I can't even hear sirens. Fuck it. I pull my grey t-shirt up over my nose and go for it. The first step into the building isn't bad but I'm quickly having to fight my way blindly through the black smoke. The heat hits me straight away, my face feels like it's blistering, and the smoke irritates my throat making me cough and fight for breath. I can barely see so much as a foot in front of my face, everything is so fogged up with smoke.

A small gap clears through the fog, enough for me to make out a hallway with doors to classrooms on either side.

"CASEY!" I call out, praying she's in one of the closest rooms, but after several seconds there's nothing.

I peer through doors; there are bags and books chaotically laying around, but I can't see a little girl.

The flames at the end of the hallway are the worst in the building, it's not hard to work out that the fire broke out in that direction. The orange flames dance up door frames, covering the ceiling and travelling towards me.

"CASEY! I'm here to help you!" Before I finish, I hear terrified sobs coming from towards the flames.

I take a few steps closer, fighting the thick smog that is choking me.

"Casey, my name is Hendrix, do you think you can keep calling my name until I find you?"

There's a short silence before I hear my name being called between sobs.

"Well done Casey, that's brilliant, keep going, okay..."

She does as I ask and with each call, I'm able to pinpoint where she could be. Behind the flames is a storage cupboard; I think she's in there. A few more steps closer and I'm hearing her clearly and loudly – she hid in the cupboard.

As I go to open the door, I gasp in pain. The fire has heated up the doorknob, making it impossible to touch.

"Hendrix?" the little girl calls again, this time with urgency. My reaction to burning my hand must have scared her.

I grit my teeth, cover my hand with my t-shirt and pull hard on the doorknob until the door swings open, and I see a little blonde curly-haired girl tucked up in the corner of the cupboard cradling her knees under her chin.

"Hey Casey, it's okay now..." She immediately leaps towards me, wrapping her arms tightly around my neck.

"I got you sweetheart, let's go find Mommy now."

It's somewhat easier heading back out since I know it's just a straight hallway, but the lack of clean oxygen makes every step feel like a mile. I realise I'm getting lightheaded, but I know I have to push through, I have this innocent kid relying on me. Her grip tightens around my neck as we step through the worst of the smoke which is making everything so dark. She must be terrified, poor kid.

It's a relief when I see some daylight drifting in and I know I'm nearly out of here. Good thing too because I feel as though my legs are ready to buckle beneath me, I need air.

"My baby!" I hear the mom cry out with relief as she pulls her daughter from me.

The sirens deafen me as two fire trucks grind to a halt in front of the building.

A shove to my chest startles me, it's Tucker.

"You could have been killed! You couldn't wait TWO minutes for the firefighters to get here? Stubborn jerk!"

His shove makes me lose my balance and I end up on my ass on the sidewalk. My eyes are blurry, and my chest is so tight I feel like I'm choking but this time no air is getting in. I gasp harder for air but it only makes me dizzy.

An oxygen mask is placed over my face just in time for me to pass out.

CHAPTER TWELVE

MADDISON

I wake up to eleven missed calls from Jamie and one text message from my mum.

> *Hi Maddison, please answer your phone when Jamie calls, he is worried sick. He has a horrible feeling that this trip is going to be a farce. Does everything seem legit? Are you safe? What's the hostel like?*

My cheeks flush red with anger and my heart bangs uncomfortably against my chest, making me anxious. How dare Jamie unnecessarily scare my mum like this. I hate him, I actually *hate* him. I can't let him win, today is the first full day of the trip and I'll be damned if I'm going to let him ruin it. I type out a brief text back to Mum, keeping it light but making a point to avoid the topic of Jamie.

> *Hi Mum! I'm safe! It's amazing here. Today we are off to the Georgia Aquarium which is apparently the biggest aquarium in the world! How cool is that. Hostel is clean, tour guide is great. Hannah and Poppy say hi. I'll message you in the week, love M x*

If I hadn't planned on taking several hundred photos today, I'd be turning my phone off, but I definitely want to capture every moment.

Even though it has the impressive title of being the world's biggest aquarium, I still can't get over its size. It is easily one the most impressive experiences of my life. The tunnel is huge and the amount of sea creatures is incredible. It makes me feel as though I am deep in the middle of the ocean, it is unbelievably stunning. I must have taken at least twenty photos in the aquarium alone – I'm starting to feel sorry for anyone who has to tediously scroll through these if and when I post them online!

Nearby we found a shark themed café where we ate fish tapas and drank blue slushie cocktails called Shark Fins. I have no idea what was in them, but they were definitely going straight to my head. So much so that Hannah wanted to keep the buzz going and head straight out to the bars and party. I didn't object, despite it only being four o'clock in the afternoon. We separated from the rest of our group who were following the more sensible plan of heading back to the hostel to get changed and freshen up before having a proper dinner. But hey, how many times will I be in Atlanta with my two best friends? Got to make these moments count right?

Poppy, of course, finds an LGBTQ+ bar; Hannah groans loud enough in protest to let half of Georgia know she's unimpressed about that. I, on the other hand, am more than happy to go to a bar where the number of men interested in me will likely be zero. I think Jamie has scared me off for life; my future is definitely starting to look like I'll be covered in cat hair and wreaking of cat piss.

The bar is so fun and carefree – nineties pop music blasts from the speakers around us, it's five shots for three dollars and the overall vibe is so light and friendly. Hannah drags me to the middle of the dancefloor, holding my hands and spinning me around. I catch a glimpse of Poppy behind Hannah, dancing with a short blonde-haired girl. I throw her a cheeky grin knowing full well this'll end in a kiss. Hannah playfully rolls her eyes.

"That's it! We are off to a straight bar next! I need an American man!" she declares loudly enough that Poppy and her dance partner hear. They giggle and carry on dancing without a care in the world.

"Come on slag bag, let's get another drink," I giggle and Hannah jokingly elbows me as she pretends to be offended for all of two seconds. We head to the bar where we order another five shots. Two each for us and we save one for Poppy.

A slightly slower song comes on and we notice Poppy now

has her arms wrapped around the girl's waist and they're passionately kissing on the dancefloor. You'd think they were the only ones in the room the way they're going at it.

Hannah and I step outside to the smoking area, even though neither of us smokes, but the shots are hitting us, and we need to cool down. Instead, we are welcomed by humidity and tobacco smoke.

"We didn't think this through," I giggle.

Hannah swings her arm around my shoulders.

"Oh well, if I have to sweat whilst choking on second-hand smoke, I'm happy it's with you."

Cringe-ball. But I feel the same. I feel like the weight I had been carrying has been lifted from my shoulders and for the first time in a long time I'm living for myself, surrounded by good people, making the best memories.

"You gonna be okay Mads? You know, when you have to go back home?" Her face shows genuine concern.

"I won't be getting back together with Jamie if that's what you're worried about?"

"No, God, no! I know you're not stupid. But you've not been happy back at home for a while. What are you going to do?"

I shrug. "Start again I guess." She nods reassuringly. "Think I'll go back to Uni and finish my veterinary nursing degree."

Poppy stumbles through the back door and out into the smoking area. Her smile beams from ear to ear as she spots us and she practically skips towards us holding up her phone proudly displaying the new girl's number.

"I'm taking her for lunch tomorrow before we get the coach down to Tennessee! She's such a babe! And the accent, wow just wow! I love it here already."

What an incredible twenty-four hours it's been. Next stop Tennessee.

CHAPTER THIRTEEN

HENDRIX

My eyes open slowly and the bright sunlight causes me to squint, but I see the silhouette of Savannah sitting in the chair beside me. The beeping of the machines and the strong smell of sanitiser lets me know I'm laid up in hospital. I feel sore, and my chest is still quite tight but other than that I feel okay, just tired.

"Is this the part where I ask where I am? And pretend I can't remember how awesome I am?"

"Jerk," Savannah mumbles but I can just about make out her smile.

"Is the girl okay?"

"She's great, they discharged her already. All thanks to you."

Thank God, I mumble to myself.

"She was terrified. I'm glad she's okay."

"Tucker is kinda pissed though."

"I figured; pretty sure I remember him yelling at me before I passed out."

"He just cares, and worries. You're quite stubborn you know. This whole bravado of being in the Marines and thinking you can handle anything and everything could get you hurt one day."

"I know what I'm doing," I answer flatly. If only they knew even a quarter of what I have seen at war they'd know a little fire isn't going to phase me.

Savannah goes quiet, staring blankly down at the magazine in her lap and I realise my answer was shitty and dismissive.

I lay quietly, staring at the ceiling and thinking about my life and the very few good people who are in it, Savannah being one of them. She wrote me every single week when I was in the Marines and, unlike the typical letters a lot of the other guys received, she never once asked me about what was happening out there or what the war was like, instead she just told me about everyday things back home. She told me about the farm and the concerts she and Tucker went to; she told me about the different cakes she had been baking and how good she was getting at it. It was refreshing really; I don't think I realised it at the time but actually her distractions were keeping me sane.

"Savannah, I never really thanked you for the letters…"

"Don't be silly, of course!" She briskly cuts me off as if it's no big deal.

I pause, contemplating whether I can open up any more than I just have. Before I can think, I ask her the question I have wanted to ask since her first letter arrived.

"How come you didn't once ask me about the war?"

She ponders for a moment before putting her magazine down on the table next to her.

"I needed you to remember that there was always a life waiting for you away from the violence you were living. I didn't want you to be sucked into the worst things of the world and to forget that there is still a lot of love here, even if it is just making a carrot cake and riding horses on a humid Tennessee summer's day."

"Well, it worked. I think it kept me going, hearing about the ranch and stuff. I don't know, I guess it did keep reminding me there was life beyond Afghanistan. Don't say anything to Tuck, but I was sure that as soon as I got home, I was going to kill myself. I even planned it, wrote a letter and everything…"

Savannah's face drops and she reaches across the bed for my hand, holding it tightly.

"But then I just thought if I give up now… I'll never try that carrot cake."

She laughs and I smile. "I'll get you a slice of that when you're out of here."

"Deal."

I must have fallen asleep because the next time I open my eyes it's dark outside and Savannah is gone. I must have missed dinner and I'm pretty hungry, but I don't want to make a fuss to the nurses who probably have better shit to do. I grab the remote and decide to chill with some tv instead. As I flick through the channels, an image catches my eye. I recognise the building and realise quickly it's the burned down school from town. Across the screen I read the words: *Local ex-Marine saves young girl, town brands him a hero.*

The next segment shows a woman with a microphone standing outside the school and referring to me again as a hero. Then a photo of my father pops up onto the screen and I feel sick. They're telling everyone how I am the son of Dawson, the heroic firefighter of 9/11.

She talks about how he tried to save my mom and discusses their death; she hails him a hero before calling me it again. I can't cope with that word. I can't deal with some fucking news reporter telling the whole town who my dad was. I came here for a fresh start, not to be followed by my past.

Fuck this. I grab at the IV tube in my arm and pull it out, ignoring the blood that spills as a result of it being snatched away too quickly. I throw on my cargo trousers and t-shirt just as the nurse enters the room and looks at me horrified.

"You can't be out of bed yet. The doctor needs to see you in the morning before you can go home."

"I'm discharging myself."

I step around her and leave before she has a chance to stop me. I don't mean to be rude to her but if I don't get out now, I fear I'll have another one of those fucking panic episodes.

I walk back to town like a man on a mission, stopping at the liquor store along the way for a bottle of whiskey. I sip it as I walk, hoping that each chug will burn away the thoughts of my dad and 9/11.

The closer I get to town the more my legs feel weak beneath me. The booze has hit me quickly, and I feel weird. I'm quite breathless and it becomes clear that maybe it was far too soon to be walking around like this. The thought of my body being weak makes me feel frustrated, and the thought of the news makes me angry; everything starts building up inside of me again. I feel like I could punch a wall repeatedly until I break my fist and still feel no relief. I feel like I have all this rage inside me, and I can feel it bubbling over, trying to escape.

The black mist comes down and I can't think straight. I feel like I could go to the bridge and throw myself off it, anything to give me peace from this fucking pain again and again. Why does this thought of taking my own life keep coming around and around? Why does it keep feeling like my only solution? Without thinking, I'm headed to the bridge, it's like my feet are doing all the thinking for me and now all I can see myself doing is standing at the edge, seconds away from ending it all.

I pull out my phone and my thumb scrolls for the therapist I swore I didn't need anymore.

She answers with a mixture of tiredness and panic. It's stupid o'clock but I didn't think.

"Help me, please," I cry. "Help me."

CHAPTER FOURTEEN

MADDISON

I'm full on in my feels as country music plays into my ears just as our coach arrives in Nashville, Tennessee. Chris Stapleton, Luke Combs and Morgan Wallen are making me want to throw on a cowboy hat and go horse riding. Tennessee has been on my bucket list for as long as I can remember, I'm in awe of everything about it. The music culture mostly but also the smaller suburban towns which seem to have remained a little more stripped back and relaxed compared to where I come from. Our town is crazy busy, everyone commuting in and out of London, staring down at their phones, rushing around and stressed out, not really living in the moment anymore; it's sad, even for a nineties kid who can just about remember simpler times.

I used to fantasise as a kid that one day I'd have my own land and surround myself with animals. Bliss. I hate to be that person who reckons they prefer animals to humans, but I do find animals easier to deal with, you know what you're getting with them. Plus, have you ever had a dog that is just so insanely happy to see you when you come home that they do a little excitable wee? That shit is magical. I start wondering whether that feeling is possible with a man. Not saying I want a boyfriend who will piss on the carpet as soon as he sees me, but how incredible to have that type of love, where them returning home is the highlight of your day. How incredibly romantic must it be to have that type of connection with another person.

"What are you smiling at?" Hannah mouths over my music to me.

Great, I can hardly tell her I was daydreaming about a man pissing on my carpet because then I'd have to explain how

I got to this weird thought in the first place, and I can't be bothered to do that.

"Just excited for Tennessee," I say instead.

It's hardly a lie though to be fair, I really am excited; in fact, I spend the remaining thirty minutes of the journey looking up the best bars for live country music on Google. There are so many! I just know this is going to top any nightlife I have ever experienced.

It's a shame we aren't spending longer here, we only have three nights. After this we visit Mississippi, then New Orleans, Alabama and lastly Florida. According to the itinerary, most of our time is spent in Florida – we have stops in Jacksonville, Orlando and Miami, bringing us to a total of ten days there. Florida is where Hannah is most excited to go, she reckons she's going to find an extremely rich man in Miami who will whisk her off her feet and give her the American dream – a multi-million-dollar beach house and a life better than the Kardashians'.

Thinking about it, Florida is Poppy's favourite place to visit as well; she tells me that Miami is the gay capital of America, after San Francisco of course, and she is so excited to experience everything it has to offer. I feel bad because she often asks me to tag along with her to a few gay bars back in London and I usually have to say no because Jamie isn't keen on me going out in London, or anywhere for that matter. I have had to say no a lot and that makes me feel bad. I make a promise to myself that when we get to Miami, I'll be the best wing woman she's ever had.

"Fuck off, this place is hilarious!" Poppy chuckles as we plonk our bags down in our room. It's all cowboy themed – hilariously over the top and kind of tacky but it's brilliant. There are pictures of rodeos and cowboys dotted around the room and the wallpaper is a retro mustard colour with pictures of cowboys swinging ropes around horses; even the hands on the clock are mini cowboy boots.

I take a good seven or eight photos of course.

"You're so camera happy," Hannah says but with a tone like it's a bad thing. Hannah doesn't take pictures unless it's of herself in an influencer style pose where she's looking candidly out into the distance or in an expensive bikini with the perfect hair and make-up.

"Speaking of pictures," she continues, "we need to do something about your Instagram. I feel like you can tell a lot about a person from their Instagram. For example, mine says…"

"I love myself?" Poppy sarcastically interrupts.

"No! It says…" She stands straight with her chest puffed out, overly confident and assertive. "It says, here's Hannah, a girl you either wish you were or a girl you wish you could date. She likes the finer things in life. That way I'll only attract the men who can actually give me that."

"Okay, so what does mine say about me?"

Hannah grabs my phone and scrolls impatiently through my grid posts. She rolls her eyes at a few – she doesn't have to say it, but I know full well they'll be the selfies I took with the cats and dogs at my veterinary placement.

"It says: I wear jumpers with cats on them."

"Fuck off!" I snort. "It does not!"

"It does a bit, where's all the sexy photos of you looking ten out of ten?"

"I don't really take those kinds of pictures."

She frowns immediately. "Cut the bullshit."

"Okay, okay, Jamie didn't like me posting them. He says it looks odd to post those kinds of pictures whilst you're in a relationship."

Hannah doesn't look the least bit surprised. Poppy looks sad. "Every girl deserves to post a photo they look beautiful in," she says.

Hannah nods enthusiastically.

"Although some women should post a lot less," Poppy smirks.

"Don't be silly!" Hannah snorts. "You can never post too many selfies."

"I beg to differ. In fact, here's a challenge for you both. Hannah, for the rest of this holiday you can only take photos of things you care about – and that doesn't include your face.

Mads, you have to take at least one banging photo of yourself every three days and upload it."

Hannah bursts out laughing, gleefully clapping her hands.

"Yes, yes! I love that so much! In fact, we HAVE to start tonight."

I fiddle with my hair, uncertain if this is a good idea. I can imagine this sending Jamie into a frenzy, and he'll just start calling me all over again, or worse, he'll call my mum.

"I don't think I even brought anything particularly sexy with me."

"You're joking?" Hannah gawps.

"Yeah, seriously Mads, you've got a banging body with the sexiest curves! How could you not have brought a figure-hugging dress or at least a low-cut top to show it all off?"

I shrug but inside I'm realising I've slowly been changing my style. Fucking hell, imagine if I had become Jamie's wife? I'd be dressing like someone from *Little House on the Prairie* before I was forty.

"Right, clearly, we have no choice. We're going shopping," Hannah announces as she grabs her bag and pulls me up from my bed by the hand.

I protest a little, but the thought of visiting a few country-style stores excites me.

"Fine, can we find an outfit to match these?" I say, as I proudly hold up the cowboy boots from my suitcase causing the girls to squeal with excitement.

"Fuck YES!" Poppy jumps up from the bed. "I love a girl in cowboy boots."

"I knew our Mads had to be in there somewhere," Hannah says, nodding approvingly.

And with that, we seem to be on a mission to find me the best outfit for my model-style photo shoot.

CHAPTER FIFTEEN

HENDRIX

Four hours I have been on this FaceTime call with Dr Edwards. Four. She stayed on the phone until I got back to the house. Thankfully Savannah and Tucker were asleep, and I've managed not to wake them. I have cried. I have rambled on to the point I don't think I made a single bit of sense. I have thrown up. I have sobered up, and now I'm embarrassed. The last time I cried I was eight years old, and it was the day I learned I lost my parents.

"It's not a weakness to cry, you understand that don't you Hendrix?"

"With all due respect ma'am, a crying man in the Marines *was* a weak man."

"You're not in the Marines anymore though and I think that this is why you've been able to cry. Your emotions have caught up with you and it is healthy to grieve now."

This is probably the tenth time she has reminded me that I'm no longer in the Marines, as if I'm unaware. I know I'm home safe and sound and I have to immerse myself back into a normal routine, but it's not that simple – to spend years seeing violence and being violent and then to be expected to just switch up and become some pillar of the community.

"I grieved for my parents," I inform her.

"I'm not necessarily talking about that grief; people grieve over all types of things. Perhaps you're grieving over your time in the Marines and that it is now over. It's also highly likely you're grieving over what you saw, from your friend Martinez."

"That asshole is not my fucking friend."

"Not now, but he was, so maybe you're grieving for him too."

I shake my head as if to bat away the thoughts of Martinez. I can't even contemplate how I could have ever been friends with such a scumbag. I'm so fucking mad at myself for that.

"Whatever, I just need you to fix me. How do we do that?"

"Well, we need to go right back to the beginning, find out where the triggers start. For instance, why is it so painful for you to be called a hero? Why is it that people wanting to celebrate you like they did your dad is so hard for you?"

"I don't know."

"But you do Hendrix, come on…"

I drop my head into my hands, sighing heavily. I don't know what she wants me to say; she thinks I'm concealing the answer, but the truth is I don't know why I feel the way I do. Every time I try to think of the reason, my mind goes blank. It's like my thoughts are too blurred to read.

"What feeling do you get when people call you a hero, or compare you to your dad? Is your response because you're angry he died? Are you angry at the way he died?"

"I don't know."

"Why are you more triggered at your dad dying but not your mom?"

I shrug again, but this time impatiently. "I don't know." And I really fucking don't.

"Ok, let's try something. Close your eyes and clear your mind. You're at the beach, nobody else is there, it's just you; you are sitting on the warm sand listening to the waves. Get comfortable."

I balance the phone on my chest as I lay back on the sofa, hearing her instructions through the speaker.

"I'm going to ask you a series of questions and without thinking I just want you to say the first thing that comes to your mind, okay?"

"Hmm-mm," I mumble, keeping my eyes closed.

"What's your favourite sandwich?"

"Pastrami."

"What's your favourite candy?"

"M&Ms."

"How old are you?"

"Thirty."

"What colour is your hair?"

"Dark brown."

"Where were you born?"

"New York."

"Do you watch football?"

"Yes."

"Who do you support?"

"The Giants."

"What's your favourite food?"

"Burgers."

"What's your middle name?"

"Dawson."

"Is that after your dad?"

"Yes."

"Is he a hero?"

"No."

"Why?"

"He left me alone."

"How?"

"He chose Mom over me."

"Keep your eyes closed and keep listening to the waves. I'm going to count back from five and when I get to one, you can open your eyes."

I listen carefully and when I hear one, I open my eyes and stare blankly at the ceiling. I think about what I said and for the first time something makes sense.

"How do you feel about what you said Hendrix?"

I clear my throat, sitting up a little.

"I feel like it makes me a jerk."

Dr Edwards laughs softly. "It doesn't, it actually makes you human. Which is probably the first glimpse I have had of that in over a year now."

"Why are you smiling?"

"Because you're one tough nut to crack, but this is a major breakthrough, even if it doesn't feel like it."

My hand reaches to the back of my neck, trying to soothe the ache. If anything, I feel worse than before.

"Hendrix, you were a little boy who needed a parent. To lose both at such a young age is unbearably cruel. You are right, your dad made a split-second decision to go into a burning building knowing there were risks. It is completely okay for you to resent that."

"But he tried to save my mom. How can I be angry at him for that? She deserved saving."

"Of course she did, but if he had stayed off duty and stayed away from the building, like he was asked, you would still have had a parent. You wouldn't have had to move away to live with your grandma and your life would have been better for it. So, you're allowed to feel angry at that."

I suddenly feel exhausted. Like this conversation has drained all of the energy I had left.

"And I think being called a hero triggers you because it makes you think of your dad, and the huge consequences he caused to your life when he tried to be a hero. And I think that really hurts you."

I grimace. "So I'm angry at a dead guy?"

"In a sense, and we can work through that, but you have got to know it's okay."

I nod appreciatively.

This has been *a lot.* Whether we call it an epiphany or a breakthrough, it wasn't easy to get here and I feel like I need a moment, not to run away, but to catch my breath.

"I think I'm going to go away for a few days, by myself. I just need to process this without everyone around me."

"And that's understandable. Where will you go?"

"Nashville probably, I'll get a hotel or something."

Dr Edwards pauses as she stares at me with deep thought.

"Do I need to be concerned that Nashville is going to be a place you'll use for round-the-clock drinking and that you'll be calling me again in a state?"

I laugh. "No ma'am, I'll go and do touristy shit or something."

"Okay, and when you come back, there are some exercises we can use to try and help you. After that, we'll move on to discussing things you told me about Martinez."

"With all due respect, I never want to hear that name again. I won't be discussing anything about him with you or with anyone else, ever. I'm sorry."

CHAPTER SIXTEEN

MADDISON

Who'd have thought shopping was so tiring, even for us girls who usually love it. I'm definitely blaming the heat and humidity for this one. But despite that, we found the coolest store only a ten-minute walk away with all sorts of flamboyant touches on typical cowboy style clothes. Even Hannah was impressed, and she usually refuses to entertain anything that's not Chanel or Gucci. We did a full-on *Say Yes to the Dress*-style catwalk, where I'd come out in a different outfit and the girls would act as my entourage and rate it out of ten.

Eventually we settled on a very cool black two-piece outfit with a belt buckle. The top part is a low-cut crop which ties at the front; it has silver tassels across the back and along both the sleeves. The second part is high-waisted panties with fishnet tights to match – they're going to look so great with the cowboy boots. Never in a million years did I think I would choose an outfit like this, especially with the amount of criticism Jamie has given my figure – but if you can't dress like a sexy cowgirl in Nashville, where can you? Poppy bought a rainbow-coloured cowboy hat, which she says she's going to add to some ripped jeans and a white corset top; she's definitely going to look so chic and pretty. Hannah bought a fringed pink top with a cowboy hat to match; she's going for a typically girly look, and she pulls it off so well.

We return to the hostel and find the itinerary for Nashville has been taped to our door. I literally jump up and down like a big kid when I read that we are off to The Country Music Hall of Fame tomorrow.

"Oh, I love that!" Poppy squeals. "That's where there's a whole Dolly Parton tribute!"

I can feel the energy shift almost instantly – the thought of going out and partying isn't as appealing as an early night to get ready for this.

"Yeah, I want to be fresh for this!" I confirm eagerly. "Early night tonight and Broadway Street tomorrow?" We agree on the plan and get ourselves to bed.

***

After a restful sleep, I'm the first awake and I have a real spring in my step – I couldn't be more excited for the day ahead if I tried. The sun is shining, the temperature is a bearable thirty degrees and the sky is blue without a cloud in sight: it couldn't be more perfect. I gather my clothes and tiptoe to the communal bathroom to get washed and changed. Hannah and Poppy are still sleeping soundly.

It's not the most glamorous bathroom in the world, but it doesn't put a dampener on my mood. I quite like what I see when I catch my reflection in the little cracked mirror above the sink – my skin looks clear and fresh, my ashy blonde highlights have gone a little brighter from the sun and my skin has a warm glow to it, making it really stand out against my chocolate hair. Crazy what a little vitamin D can do.

I put on the lightest bit of make-up and run some mousse through my hair and scrunch up the ends, allowing it to be its wavy and natural self. I pull on some blue denim shorts, a white tank top and my white Converses and I'm ready for the day.

"Wow, you are eager!" Hannah's voice groans from under her duvet.

"Aren't you? A day exploring a museum dedicated to incredible music, followed by a night out on Broadway Street? Think of the cocktails we'll be sipping later."

"Think of the men," Poppy interjects which makes Hannah sit bolt upright in bed.

"Okay, I'm eager now, I'm getting ready."

By the time Hannah finishes putting the final curl through her long blonde hair, the rest of us including the tour guide are already gathered and waiting outside.

"What?" Hannah shrugs as she coolly pops on her shades

without a care in the world.

"You're going to have to do a shot tonight for every minute you were late. That's the new deal," Poppy demands, wagging her finger in her face jokingly.

"Fine," she smirks, completely unphased.

I worry far too much to ever be like Hannah but that doesn't stop me from wishing I could be more relaxed like her. I could never rock up somewhere fifteen minutes late without frantically apologising. Hannah, however, flicks her hair over her shoulder, gets on the coach and pays zero attention to the people who are rolling their eyes at her poor punctuality.

The museum isn't far from the hostel and, as I expected, Hannah gets bored pretty quickly and she and Poppy end up wandering off on their own. I, however, stay close to the tour guide like a complete nerd, taking three hundred photos of every little thing and wishing I had someone to send them to. It blows my mind to be so close to outfits worn by Elvis Presley in his prime and to see a guitar once owned by Johnny Cash. I feel so grateful to be here. Every little artifact and piece of memorabilia mesmerises me.

After being gone for a good hour, Poppy and Hannah suddenly appear out of nowhere, giggling loudly and practically swaying.

"There she bloody is!" Hannah points.

"Are you guys drunk!?"

"They had free whiskey samples in the gift shop, they're STRONG!" They both fall about laughing at Hannah's attempt to talk without slurring. Jesus Christ, that is some strong whiskey.

Hannah rolls her eyes when she realises the camera app is open on my phone.

"God, I didn't realise you'd be THIS interested in the museum."

"What can I say? Without Jamie I'm suddenly enjoying life. Literally loving every minute of this."

"You sound like a hippy!" Poppy giggles.

"You're right, I should join a cult now and change my name to Ocean or something."

The pair keep giggling like naughty schoolgirls and I can't help but laugh with them. They're in no fit state to continue with the tour though and it's only two o'clock in the afternoon.

"Come on, shall we get back to the hostel and get into our outfits?"

Hannah's face lights up. "Already?"

"Sure, why not? You're both halfway drunk already, we may as well continue!"

"I knew she was my best friend for a reason! Let's go!" Hannah practically ushers me through the door and before we know it, we are in an Uber headed back to the hostel to get ready for a night out in Nashville.

I feel a little out of my comfort zone once I'm in my outfit – I might need a vodka or two just for some courage. I still love it though; I love the way it hugs my curves, but I haven't worn anything like this in so long that I'm doubting myself a little bit.

"Stop it," Hannah pipes up, disturbing my negative thoughts.

"Stop what?"

"Wondering whether you should be wearing that outfit. You bought it because it looks made for you. You're banging, you're a bloody ten out of ten. Got it?"

"Yeah Mads! If you weren't my friend, I'd be totally hitting on you tonight!" Poppy adds with a ridiculously cringey wink. She cracks me up.

I stare back at my reflection. I do like how my bum and boobs look in it; my thighs are a little chubby, but I don't mind them. I have kept my hair wavy and natural but added some more make-up, I have natural lash extensions on and go for a bold red lipstick.

"Okay, stop staring at yourself, let's go out and get that photo."

Oh shit, the Instagram thirst trap. I forgot.

"Don't over think it either Miss! Let's go." Poppy tugs me

by the arm and we head straight out onto the streets of Nashville. It's late afternoon now, the sun is a little lower in the sky, the air is still warm and humid but with a gentle breeze.

As we approach Broadway Street, Poppy stops us in our tracks. "This is it!" she says excitedly. "You need to stand here, in this spot – behind you, all the lights from the bars and neon signs will blur a little and it'll look so cool!"

Before I can say a word, Hannah is ushering me to the right spot and Poppy has my phone and is angling the camera to capture my best side.

"Need more light," Poppy calls out like a director on the set of an important movie.

"Got it!" Hannah pulls out her phone and puts the flash on, holding it up high next to Poppy so it brightens my face.

"Pose like a confident Queen!" Hannah calls, totally making this awkward, but sod it! I giggle nervously, then place one hand on my hip, my other high in the air to show off the amazing scene behind me, one leg is slightly in front, leaning my hip to the side.

Poppy takes a few photos before pausing.

"Fuck off! I have the BEST photo ever."

Hannah peers over her shoulder with a huge smile, impressed at what she sees.

Before I even get to see it, Poppy captions it and proudly posts it.

"Wait, shit! Did you actually post that without me seeing it?"

"Yep!" she answers, sounding so pleased with herself. She holds my phone in front of my face. The caption reads *I think Nashville looks good on me #nashville #travelling.*

I can't lie, the shot is incredible. The lights behind me have blurred slightly just like she predicted, making it look really candid and fun, but it's me I can't take my eyes off. The lighting makes my skin look like it's glowing, I look so happy, my smile is so wide and authentic. My body looks tanned, and the clothes do look made for me. This is quite possibly the best photo I have seen of myself in years. I feel beautiful. And not in a 'you look beautiful, but...' kind of way. I just look, well, banging, as my friends would say.

CHAPTER SEVENTEEN

HENDRIX

Tucker looks concerned about my last-minute trip to Nashville.

"But your new home is ready tomorrow. Why don't you just stay? You'll have your own space then," Tucker points out.

"I know and I'm happy about that, but I've just got to get out of town for a day or two whilst I sort myself out. I can't be around people calling me a hero right now, it's hard to explain but trust me."

He looks disappointed, like I'm giving up on my new life in Tennessee already, but I'm not. I know I'll be happier here, but it'll take time. Savannah comforts her husband by putting her hand across his shoulder blade.

"Sounds like a great idea. Things have been a little overwhelming here, I think a reset will be just what you need." She says it more to reassure Tucker than to agree with me, but I appreciate it anyway.

"Fine. And when you come back, you'll avoid messing with married women and running into burning buildings?" he pleads.

"I'll try my best."

I throw a small bag into the back of my truck and start heading to a little hotel I found called The Urban Cowboy; it only has eight rooms so hopefully it'll be quiet.

A lot of my conversation with Dr Edwards replays in my head during the drive. I think about how different my life could have been if my dad had kept away from the towers; it makes me wonder – would we still have football Sundays? Would we go to the game together and watch the Giants play? Would we have bonded over football with a cold beer when I turned twenty-one?

I wonder a lot about how different life could have been for me. I love my grandma, I do, but life for a young guy was hard there. We had very little in common, I'm not religious and I had no friends. It was lonely there, I lost count of the number of times I cried myself to sleep, wishing things could have been different. I guess I understand now why I'm angry, I know things could have been so different, if only my dad had worried more about leaving me alone in this world and less about always needing to be the hero.

One thing I do remember that my sweet Grandma came up with to try and help me was getting me a journal. She told me that when my brain was too busy with thoughts, I should get them down on paper. I never did that, but I oddly have the urge to now. I stop by a store a block away from the hotel and buy myself a black journal with a matching pen.

In typical Nashville style, my room is completely over the top and cowboy themed, but the bed is comfortable, and the mini bar is stocked, so I can't complain. I sit down at the dark wooden desk with my journal and pen. Without giving it a lot of thought, I'm immediately scribbling stuff down; I fill one page and then another and another. The next time I look up from my desk it's dark outside and my eyes are heavy and my hands ache. I must have filled half the journal. I have written down everything that I have been holding in about missing my mom, being mad at my dad, struggling as a kid, everything. Between this and the long call with my therapist last night I'm tired as hell and although I don't plan to go to sleep already, I find myself dozing off in the chair.

CHAPTER EIGHTEEN

MADDISON

The night is in full swing. Hannah bought a whole tray of shooters for ten bucks, and I got us a yard of beer each. By the time we made it to the third bar we were already swaying along the strip.

"Ooh! This place has fishbowls!" Poppy squeals as she reminds us that it's her round, and we all follow on behind her into a pink bar called The Flamingo. The atmosphere is electric, and the music is loud; there's a man on the stage with a guitar singing an upbeat country song. He has a thick beard and a plaid shirt and I smile to myself at how perfectly he matches the style of this city. Three huge fishbowls arrive in front of us in no time at all with sparklers and paper decorations of cowboy boots and guitars sticking out the top.

"One EACH?" Hannah and I say in unison, our jaws dropping open.

Poppy smirks as she stares at the gigantic bowls filled with liquor and then back at us.

"In my defence I didn't realise they'd be THIS big! Oh well, get sipping girls!" She shoots us a careless wink, like we aren't about to get alcohol poisoning.

A split-second memory flashes in my mind of Jamie lecturing me about drinking cocktails, moaning at me about the amount of sugar that'll sit on my hips and make me appear bigger and how damaging that is to his brand.

"Dickhead," I mumble to myself as I throw out the straw from the bowl and lift it to my lips instead and start chugging away.

"Dickhead?" Hannah looks confused but Poppy informs her that I probably just had a Jamie flashback.

"This is why you need to hurry up and be a goddam therapist!" I shout, in between chugs.

The girls seem particularly impressed at my chugging and both throw out their straws to copy me.

"Am I going to have to keep an eye on you girls?" an attractive bartender calls over the music. Of course, Hannah flicks her hair back over her shoulders, enjoying the extra attention.

"I sure hope so," she says smoothly. I swear, the majority of us could only dream of flirting in the way Hannah does. She's so effortless with it, relaxed and carefree. If I had said that I'd be the biggest cringe ball on the planet and the poor bartender would probably just stare at me the way Napoleon Dynamite stares at Tina, the fat llama. I love that movie.

The next thing I know, I'm in the centre of the floor line dancing. Yes, line dancing. Apparently in this city everyone just knows how to line dance – we must have missed the memo because Hannah, Poppy and I mostly resemble a group of elderly ladies with vertigo. None of us are in time and we mostly stumble into other people, or worse, trip over our own feet.

Still, each time we catch each other's eyes we giggle like schoolgirls. Eventually I give up and break into the robot instead which sends Poppy into hysterics. The mix of downing half a fishbowl and attempting to line dance has caused the alcohol to rush to our heads. The disco lights that twirl around the room are making me feel dizzy, but I don't mind too much. I haven't been this drunk in so long and I just decide to enjoy the moment. Soon, most of the line dancers have gone back to their seats and it's just me and Poppy left doing a mixture of the robot and some new TikTok trend that she has been trying and failing to teach me.

"I'm going outside for a smoke!" Poppy mouths over the music and I take that as my cue to take a quick toilet stop. As I sit swaying on the toilet, having the longest pee in history, I suddenly wonder how my Instagram post is doing, plus it's an excuse to look at the photo I'm now vainly obsessed with. Before I can even open the app, I see that my phone screen is plagued with message notifications from Jamie. None of them are particularly nice but they slowly get worse. I can sense how angry he is becoming with each message.

Maddy, call me asap.

Mads, that photo is NOT you.

Maddison, take down that photo, you look desperate. I'm only saying it because I care.

Maddison call me back please.

Maddison why are you trying to look like a desperate slag? Did Hannah put you up to this?

Maddison for fuck's sake, call me back.

Maddison why would you wear that outfit? It's embarrassing.

I'm embarrassed for you at this point, I really am.

My eyes begin to water causing the words blur through the tears.

Suddenly, my phone starts vibrating in my hand. It's Jamie. I'm so angry and hurt by his messages that I don't hesitate to answer, I'll quite happily give him a piece of my mind.

"Hello?" I slur.

"Fantastic, thought you must have been drunk to post a photo like that! Do you know what kind of men you'll attract with a slutty image like that?"

I swallow hard, attempting to compose myself so he doesn't hear the catch in my throat from crying.

"Hopefully one who is better than you!"

"Excuse me?"

"This is the space I have needed to realise you have been putting me down for longer than I care to admit, and I have just stayed and put up with it. I have tried to better myself for you, but I deserve to feel good enough!" The emotions catch me by surprise, and it ends up clear I am crying.

"So, we are DONE Jamie, do you understand? Now leave me alone!"

Jamie pauses. I can hear him breathing but he isn't saying anything. I wait patiently for him to call me a slag again or maybe even agree to leave me alone, but nothing. Just as I prepare to hang up, he speaks.

"Ask Hannah how many times we fucked behind your back."

The line goes dead.

CHAPTER NINETEEN

HENDRIX

I wake up confused to find I'm still sitting at the desk – that had to be one of the best fucking naps I have ever had. Grandma was right, getting all that shit down on paper really helped clear my mind and took a weight off my shoulders. The clock on the bedside table shows that it's almost midnight now but I feel wide awake. I doubt I'll fall back to sleep, and I don't fancy just lying on the bed staring up at the ceiling for hours on end either.

But this is Nashville, there is always something open.

I decide that I'm going to brush my teeth, throw on a new shirt and go for a drink. In fact, I think my first drink will be a toast to Grandma – who'd have thought her advice from all those years ago would apply to me so well now?

By the time I get to Broadway Street, the place is bustling with a lot of drunk bachelor and bachelorette parties. It's maybe a little more than I am in the mood for right now. Instead, I decide to head away from the street and see if I can find something a little quieter. As luck would have it, I find an old sports bar at the bottom of the hill; it's certainly outdated and could use a lick of paint but it's far more relaxed with a lot fewer people and that's just what I want. I grab a stool at the bar and order myself a bowl of nachos and a whiskey. The vibe is casual and easy, no loud bands or groups of people playing drinking games, just a few screens showing sports highlights and a couple of guys chatting over their beers.

The nachos go down a treat, I hadn't realised how hungry I had gotten. I decide to shoot Tucker a text message, even though it's late I'm sure he'll appreciate knowing I haven't got into any more fights and I'm not drinking myself stupid.

Hey Tuck, Nashville is good. I ended up taking a piece of Grandma's advice and I'm feeling better already. See you in a day or two.

Within a second, I get a message back.

Grandma's been dead years, how many have you had?!?

His banter makes me smile and although I'm not one for emojis, I send back a crying laughing face.

I relax into my seat, watching the NFL highlights and slowly sipping at my whiskey; this is the most relaxed I have felt since leaving the Marines. I really do feel like I'm finally regaining some normality. I don't feel on edge or ready to fight, I actually feel keen to get back to the ranch soon. I want to help Tucker fix up the barn and the key to my lodge is ready. I'm not into interior design but there's a few things that need fixing up and sorting. It'll be good for me to get it how I want.

"Another whiskey, sir?" the bartender asks as I finish my last sip.

"Yes please, oh wait, actually, I'll have a Diet Coke." I need to drink less and keep my mind sharp and now seems as good a time as any to apply that.

CHAPTER TWENTY

MADDISON

I suddenly feel so awkward and exposed in what I'm wearing and I'm wishing so much I had a jacket with me. I stare at myself in the mirror, mascara streaks staining my cheeks, my eyes puffy from crying so much and I feel so embarrassed and stupid that I wish I could click my fingers and be in my bed, under the safety of my duvet and not stood here looking like something from a horror movie. I have to get out of here and now.

I march out of the toilets and across the dancefloor. I have the exit in my view and I'm gunning for it, but before I'm out, Hannah steps in front of me.

"Woah! What happened in there!?" She stares blankly at me before trying to wipe away a tear, but I shove her hand away.

"How many times?"

"What?"

"How many times did you sleep with my boyfriend behind my back? How many times did you screw me over?"

The colour drains from her face and she looks guilty as hell. It's not like Hannah to be speechless but I can clearly see her scrambling to find the right words.

"He, I… It was just a few."

"Just a few." I laugh in her face. "That's okay then, if it was *just* a few."

"I just meant…"

"How could you do this? You hate Jamie! It makes no sense."

She looks awkwardly at the floor.

"Oh, you don't hate Jamie, do you?"

She pauses, not answering me which speaks volumes in itself.

"So, you've been pretending to hate him? So, why? So that I wouldn't click on? Or so I would leave him quicker?"

She shrugs, still not saying a word.

"Well, you can have him." I storm past her and out the door. Just when I think I'm free, Poppy tugs me by the arm.

"Hey you! Where are you going?"

She stops smiling when she sees my smudged make-up and watery eyes.

"Mads? What's wrong?"

"I thought she was my best friend!" I sob into her shoulder. "She was sleeping with Jamie behind my back this whole time."

"She finally told you!?" Poppy pulls me in, hugging me tightly.

I pull away, clicking at what she said.

"*Finally?* Did you know?"

"She asked me not to tell you! She said she would do it in her own time. I didn't really want to get involved."

I straighten myself out, wiping my eyes and composing myself.

"Some best friends you both turned out to be," I say calmly, spinning on my heel and walking away quickly before either of them can try to catch up with me. I hear Poppy calling after me, shouting for me to stop and go back but I ignore her.

I'm walking so fast that I feel as though my legs could fall off, but I feel a lot better when I turn to see the bright lights of Broadway Street are now long gone into the distance. I need a drink, a stiff drink, and then I need to make a plan. What the hell am I supposed to do from here?

I can't go home, I don't want to be near Jamie, in a place that has brought me so much unhappiness. And I'm definitely not about to continue on this trip with Hannah and Poppy, there is no way in hell that could work. I'm screwed. I'm out of options and I'm stuck.

I stumble into the first bar I find that seems quieter. I need a drink. I need a plan.

CHAPTER TWENTY-ONE

HENDRIX

Unexpectedly, a woman stumbles through the door and into the bar. I think it's mostly unexpected for everyone else because she's a woman and this bar doesn't look like it sees many females. But for me, it's how sad she looks. Her eyes look sore and strained and she looks as though she is visibly trembling. I almost want to ask her if she's okay, even though it's painfully obvious that she's not, but I have a feeling she'll tell me to mind my own business.

"Broadway Street is at the top of the hill, ma'am," the bartender informs her. It's a fair assumption, she is dressed like she was a part of one of the many bachelorette parties that happen up there.

"I've just come from there. It wasn't my cup of tea. Can I have a vodka and Diet Coke please." She surprises me by answering him politely in a British accent. I watch as her trembling hands pick up a napkin and she starts dabbing her face, cleaning up some of the make-up under her eyes. She takes a seat on the stool next to mine but pays no attention to me or anyone else, only the barman.

Then I realise I'm staring for another reason. She's beautiful. She has this honest innocence about her which makes her angelic. Fuck off, what am I saying? I don't think I have used that word in my life. Although there's also an edge to her I realise when I see what looks like a cherry blossom tattoo across her shoulder. Somehow, she's even more beautiful now. Innocent but with an edge. Interesting.

She drinks her vodka whilst looking deep in thought, her body still slightly trembling.

"Okay, you can't be cold in this humidity, so I feel the need to ask if you're okay because you're shaking a hell of a lot." It just slips out, but I have said it now. Thankfully she doesn't tell me to mind my own business. She turns to look at me; her eyes travel up and down my body momentarily before she answers.

"I'm not cold, but I can't stop shaking. It's been a rough night and I just hate what I'm wearing right now."

"You hate what you're wearing?" I look her up and down in disbelief – has the girl not seen herself in the mirror? This is the type of outfit people throw on to be trashy and have fun, but she pulls it off so much better than them, she looks classy but sexy as hell. The pants hug the curve in her hips like they were made for her.

Before she responds, I take off my shirt. I have a black tank top underneath, so I don't mind. I hand it to her; she takes it suspiciously at first but when she locks eyes with me, she smiles.

"Thank you…" she answers gratefully as she slides her arms into the sleeves and buttons up the front before knocking back the last of her vodka.

"You want another?"

She frowns and looks me up and down again, this time suspiciously.

"I'm not into one-night stands." Her answer throws me off guard a little.

"Shit, I didn't even know I asked! Or is it a vibe I give off? You better tell me what it is before I end up going home with one of those old guys!" I joke, gesturing to the elderly gentlemen still deep in chat over their beers. She glances at them quickly before giggling. Progress, I think, I have her laughing and she's stopped shaking now.

She nods, so I order her a vodka and myself another Diet Coke.

"So, what brings you to Nashville?"

"I came with my best friends. Well…" She pauses, looking like she might cry all over again.

"It's too long a story," she says instead.

I honestly can't explain why, but I want to listen to everything she has to say and understand how she has got to this moment, crying alone in an old bar.

"Well, lucky for you I've not long woken up so I'm in no rush to be anywhere."

"I honestly don't know where to start. Have you ever just felt so lost?"

I understand that feeling more than I can say, but right now it's about her and not me. It's funny because talking to an emotional woman in a bar would usually be the last thing I'd want to do. I'd probably catch a chick crying like this and assume she's having some bullshit drama with her douchebag boyfriend and be relieved I don't have to listen. Yet here I am, not going anywhere, fixed on her, hanging on to her every word like I need to know everything so I can help. Me, help? I can barely help myself. I'd be the world's worst person to go to for advice, but here I am, wanting to try anyway.

"I have," I manage to mumble in response.

She tosses her head back impatiently as if the thoughts in her mind throw her from sad to angry in a split second.

"I was sitting on the toilet having a pee, minding my own business and boom, my ex-boyfriend texts me to tell me I look like a slag in all my photos and that he shagged my best friend!"

I have to cover my mouth with my hand for a second so she can't see me pushing back my smile. Just when I thought she couldn't get any better, she freely tells me about all the drama that unfolded during a drunk piss.

"Okay, firstly, what's a slag?"

"Oh, you don't say that here?"

"I don't think so, but if it's the same as a slut then it's pretty obvious why he has said that."

"Is it?" She groans heavily.

"Sure, it means he feels threatened as hell and the only way he can still have any type of control over you is by putting you down, making you feel worthless and shit, probably so you don't feel confident around any other guys."

She looks as though I have perfectly hit the nail on the head. She awkwardly stares down at her lap, looking beat down.

"I was going to leave him ages ago when I realised he was affecting my confidence, but I kept putting it off because he was so busy with work. I didn't want to make his life worse, you know?"

"Not really," I answer honestly. "I've been doing things for myself for as long as I can remember. Do you often put other people first like that? Because if so, that's concerning, we need to get you to a doctor, maybe he can give you a pill or something." Her mouth widens as she giggles. I focus on her smile and the way it brings her face to light, beautiful.

"Maybe I do need a pill. He was one of the worst decisions I ever made. And on top of that I have two best friends who both lied and betrayed me."

"Now that's why I don't have friends. Well, I have Tucker but he's my cousin, so he has to tolerate me. Other than that, I prefer to be on my own, it's easier that way, no one can let you down."

As the words leave my mouth I wonder if that was the best advice.

"I'm not saying to cut everybody off and become a recluse…"

"No, maybe that's exactly what I should do."

She orders two shots of whiskey and without hesitation she makes a toast.

"To being your own best friend." She smiles confidently and clicks her glass against mine before knocking it back.

Her growing confidence is sexy as hell.

"So, when did you leave what's-his-face?" I ask, feeling a weird tinge of jealousy inside.

"I don't know, a month ago, but really, I think it has been dead in the water for well over six months. I gave up my career for him. God, that's another terrible decision I have made, already up to two."

"Okay, okay, pity Polly, you can't be the only one moping over decisions. Want to hear some of mine?"

She nods instantly, leaning into me.

"I moved to this small town where my cousin lives, and I accidently slept with a married woman on my first day."

"What!?" she gasps, making the whole bar turn and look.

I lean in to whisper the next part, "That's not even the worst part. Her husband, who puts up with her cheating, is battling aggressive cancer."

"No way!" She looks horrified but not in the least bit judgemental.

"Can you imagine what a jerk I feel?"

"You are a jerk!" she teases. "Ew, I'm drinking with a jerk."

"Oh really? Okay, come on then, I'll walk you back to your best friends."

"No thanks!" She giggles. "I'd rather drink with this sex-crazed jerk."

"Sex crazed?" I question and she drapes her head across my shoulder laughing.

"Well, you must be, that was pretty awful…"

"Okay, now you sound like every single person in the town."

"I mean, you kinda deserve it!"

She giggles, playfully nudging me, and this is how our conversation goes for the next drink or two, lots of laughing and teasing.

CHAPTER TWENTY-TWO

MADDISON

It's only when I catch the time on the tv screen that I realise it's almost two in the morning and the bar has pretty much emptied. I had barely noticed any of that because of how much I was waffling on.

"Wait, I don't even know your name!" I cringe at myself for talking so much that the poor guy hasn't even been able to tell me his name.

"It's Hendrix," he says with a grin, showing off his beautifully straight white teeth.

Initially, I wasn't in the mood for company, and I had been so wrapped up in myself that I wasn't fully aware of how handsome Hendrix is. He has dark hair, which is short in a simple buzz cut that really suits his face; his jaw is strong and defined and his eyes are as dark as his hair. His arms are thick and muscly, making every tattoo pop which is very visually pleasing. I try not to stare but I know he has caught me doing just that a couple of times.

"Maddison, or Maddy," I inform him.

"Ten minutes til close guys," the barman says as he collects our empty glasses.

Those five words jolt me back to reality.

"What's wrong?" Hendrix asks, staring at me with such intensity that I get butterflies in my stomach.

"It's just everything is still a mess, and I don't know what to do. I'm still lost."

"Where are you staying?"

"In some hostel near Broadway. I'm sharing a room with both Hannah and Poppy, and I just can't deal with seeing them right now." The thought of having to face Hannah makes me feel sick, I can't imagine ever being her friend again.

"Is there definitely no hope of you guys moving past this?"

I arch my brow at him. "Would you forgive your friend?"

"No, I'd probably beat his ass, but you said it yourself, they've been your friends since you were little kids."

I ponder it for a moment, but my mind is made up.

"My whole life I have put other people first and let them walk all over me. That needs to stop. There is no going back, life is too short to surround yourself with people you can't trust. I'm tired of that being my life, so tired."

He stares at me thoughtfully for just long enough that I wonder if he is about to kiss me, but instead he takes me by the hand.

"Come on, the Waffle Shack is twenty-four hours, you hungry? I'm starving." I nod, feeling quite relieved; I haven't eaten a bite since this afternoon.

The Waffle Shack is only a five-minute walk away. Hendrix strolls along closely beside me, almost as if he is protecting me from the groups of drunk men leaving the clubs. I find it quite comforting, although I can't imagine many people would want to pick a fight with Hendrix – he is tall, broad and muscly, his broad shoulders alone could make the average person look like a borrower.

I practically chew his ear off over our waffles, explaining how the thought of going home makes me desperately sad. It hasn't been a place I have been happy for a while and knowing what I now know will just make it ten times worse. I feel alone there. But I know I can't travel with the girls either.

Hendrix doesn't say much but he nods along, listening intently, eventually he places down his coffee and looks vulnerable.

"I want you to know that I know how you feel, it's the loneliest feeling in the world when you feel that lost, but I'm right there with you." He clears his throat. "The Marines was the only place I felt important. When I came out, it was the worst feeling ever. I hated going back to a place that was never home. I'd drink whiskey til I fell asleep. I mean, you know it's bad when you'd rather be in the middle of a war than inside your own four walls. So I get it, and I agree – you can't go back."

I stare down at the dog tags around his neck and kick myself for not making the connection sooner, of course he's an ex-Marine, he's built like GI Joe for fuck's sake.

"You were in the Marines? God, I have talked about myself so much, I didn't even ask about you…"

"Relax." He smiles reassuringly. "I rarely talk about it anyway."

Of course, that makes me more curious and now I have a hundred questions, but I don't want to push him; he has been nothing but courteous and I don't want to push his boundaries. I can only imagine how hard it must be, my grandad apparently didn't say a single word for two years after World War Two and we were never allowed to ask him about it.

"Anyway, you sure you don't want bacon with your waffles?"

"Firstly," I smirk, "that's not bacon. I have no idea why you call this dried-up stick bacon, but you need Jesus. And secondly, syrup and sweet waffles do NOT go with meat. You're gross!"

I love how he pretends to be insulted for a split second but really, I get the feeling he likes me challenging him.

"Ma'am, you've just offended the whole of America," he teases and throws the dry bit of bacon playfully at me.

My phone pings which stops me giggling straight away. A horrible ache forms in my stomach as I dread looking at my phone. I half expect to see some sort of apology from Hannah, but it's not her, it's Jamie.

When you've taken that photo down and apologised, we can talk about Hannah and move forward.

He must actually be insane! The arrogance of him makes me feel quite sick. How could I have been with such a narcissist? On what planet does he think I should be the one apologising?

Hendrix watches me curiously. I spin my phone around to face him. He reads the message with a twitch of the jaw, almost as if he is angry, then he laughs.

"Wow, where'd you find this guy?"

I shrug, embarrassed.

"There's a simple fix to this. I'll show you." He takes my phone, clicks on Jamie's information and then scrolls down to the block button.

I shuffle anxiously in my seat; I have never blocked someone before.

"Fixed. Now you can concentrate on yourself, without distractions." He smiles as if it was the simplest solution ever.

"Shit. What if it makes him angrier?"

Hendrix laughs. "And? You're like four thousand miles away and he can't contact you even if he is. Stop worrying about other people – that's what got you feeling so lost in the first place, remember?"

He's right, he is so right, and I should have blocked Jamie ages ago. Why didn't I even think to do it? Probably because I'm such a people pleaser, but I have to stop that. If I want to change, and I mean *really* change, I have to stop putting other people first all the time.

I smile at him gratefully.

"Okay, that's one problem solved. Now I just have to work out how to avoid Poppy and Hannah tonight."

"Oh, that's an easy one," Hendrix smiles knowingly. "We're gonna pull an all-nighter."

"An all-nighter?" I gulp, nearly choking on my coffee. I didn't even know this man a few hours ago and now I'm going to walk around a huge city with him until morning?

"Yeah, that way you don't have to deal with anything you don't want to. And I get to hang with you for longer."

I arch my brow at him. I think he just subtly paid me a compliment.

"What's going to be open at this time?"

"Well… there's the park and there's at least another four Waffle Shacks along the way so we can get a decent sugar rush going and then spend the last few hours walking it off." He says it with such sarcasm, but it actually sounds right up my street.

CHAPTER TWENTY-THREE

HENDRIX

I'm pleased when Maddison looks as impressed with the park as I am. I had never been here before, but I knew it was going to be a good place for us to walk around because I have seen tonnes of photos of Tucker and Savannah visiting here over the years. If we'd turned up to a park full of crack pipes and prostitutes I'd have been mortified. Even in the dark you can tell it's a beautiful spot. I laugh at how quick Maddison is to get her phone out and take several photos of everything she sees. I can't remember the last time I took a photo but it's endearing to see how much she enjoys it.

"I know," she sighs after catching me staring at her. "My friends moan at me all the time and tell me I take far too many photos, but I can't help it, I just love locking in a memory, you know?"

I nod, although I can't relate. "I like your way of thinking. Unfortunately, there weren't many things I wanted to take pictures of in Afghanistan."

She turns, intrigued; her eyes are burning with questions, I can tell.

"How long were you there for?"

"I joined as soon as I turned eighteen, so twelve years."

"Wow, that's a really big chunk of your life to be away," she says, heading towards a bench and sitting down. I sit in the space next to her.

"Yeah, well there wasn't much to go home for."

"Didn't your parents mind?"

"They both died when I was eight." Her face drops and of course she apologises sympathetically.

I can't help but smile as she stumbles over her words and looks painfully awkward.

"What's funny!?" she asks, embarrassed.

"You. Trying to apologise in that uptight panicky way you just did."

"Uptight?"

"You know what I mean, you really put a lot of pressure on yourself to say and do the right thing all of the time don't you?"

"Don't you?" she asks, arms folded.

"Not often, majority of the time I don't give a shit. Which I think my family are desperately hoping I improve on."

"Looks like we both have stuff to work on," she points out. I can tell she has more questions for me; she looks deep in thought.

"You can have one more question about Afghanistan if you want," I reluctantly offer. I would usually tell people to fuck off and warn them to mind their own business, but Maddison has spilled all her feelings to me tonight, I should offer something back.

She smiles gratefully.

"How about we start with your parents instead? How did they pass away?"

"9/11"

"Oh shit!" She answers with pretty much the expected reaction.

"Okay, well Afghanistan makes a lot more sense now."

I nod. "Yeah, but if anything, I came out angrier and more fucked up than before."

She doesn't say anything to that, but her eyes fix on mine, looking sad.

"Anyway, we need to sort you out. How are you feeling now?"

She pauses, pondering my question.

"I'm only sad I lost friends out of this. I'll miss Poppy the most – I love her like a sister, but I would never have allowed someone to go behind her back like this. I thought I could trust her to tell me something this big. But in the same breath, I think I'll be okay. I haven't liked my life for a while – maybe a completely fresh start is what I need."

I watch in awe of her, she's braver than most people I have met – she just picks herself up and quickly dusts herself off. I like that about her – a lot.

"So, with that said, I think I'm going to stay here for the rest of the trip. I might even see if I can extend my stay and maybe get some work as well. I'm not sure how hard that'll be though, I know there are a lot of rules about this stuff."

"In the city maybe, but in the quieter towns people will pay you cash in hand no questions asked. It's that southern hospitality."

Her face lights up with a hopeful smile.

"Okay, well that's my plan. I think I'll travel a little by myself, I really wanted to see Memphis so I might get a bus there. Then see if I can find work."

For the next half an hour she tells me all about her dream to be a veterinarian; she talks so passionately about animals but her innocence in letting all this go to help support what's-his-face makes me so frustrated for her. My grandma always used to say the kindest people can be the most vulnerable and I guess that's true here. What's-his-face screwed her over and she's paying the price.

CHAPTER TWENTY-FOUR

MADDISON

The sun begins to appear behind the trees, making the lake sparkle. I, of course, take an obscene number of photos now that it's finally light enough to capture the scenery. I can feel Hendrix's eyes on me as he watches from the bench which makes me quite flustered, although he seems to be somewhat interested which is refreshing as most people just get fed up with me being as camera happy as I am.

"Right, I need to do something crazy," I blurt.

"You mean meeting a strange man in a bar and sitting in a park with him all night wasn't crazy enough for you?"

"I didn't think of it like that. Okay, so I want to do another crazy thing. I feel like this is a moment I want to remember – the moment I cut off everyone who brings me negativity and embark on a one-woman adventure around Tennessee."

Hendrix throws his head back and lets out a deep laugh. "I mean, I'm not sure about the one-woman adventure part – you're in Nashville, not backpacking in the Amazon Rainforest *but* if it fits with what you're thinking, there's a twenty-four-hour tattoo shop a couple of blocks away. I saw it when I walked into the city."

"YES!" I practically squeal like a kid on Christmas Day. I always wanted more cute little tattoos, and this is the perfect time to get my second.

Nashville really does offer everything and before I know it, I'm sitting in a tattoo studio with black walls and loud music at six thirty in the morning picking out a tattoo. I already have an idea in mind and the tattooist is only too happy to draw something up.

"How's this?" he asks, placing a rough sketch of my quote in a beautiful cursive style with a little heart on the end.

I look at Hendrix with excitement as I get myself comfortable on the chair.

"You not having one?" I ask him, seeing as it's obvious tattoos are his thing.

He stares down at his arms. "I think I'm running out of space."

I drop my bottom lip. "Please! I can't be the only one, you must have space somewhere?"

"What, like on my ass? Cos that's where it'll have to go at this rate."

I laugh but keep my eyes scanning his body, he must have somewhere.

"How about this? It's small – you could probably fit it on the side of your thumb," the tattooist intervenes, showing us a cute cowboy hat tattoo.

"Oh my god! Yes!" I clap just as Hendrix rolls his eyes.

"Really?"

"Yes, really! That's the one."

"Fine," he agrees, sitting down on the chair beside me, "but I am not going on a one-woman adventure after this as well, okay?"

He makes me giggle. "Fine, just the tattoo for now."

Hendrix's tattoo is done within minutes; mine takes a little longer and I am quickly regretting the body part of choice. The side of my foot is extremely nippy and I'm desperately trying to take it like a pro, but the obvious gritting of my teeth is giving the game away, much to Hendrix's amusement.

A quick spray and a wipe and it's finally finished.

Never leave Nashville the same way again with a tiny heart and it's perfect.

"Very tasteful, I like it." Hendrix grins and I feel the return of butterflies swarm my stomach. I don't think he has any idea, but he is sexy as hell; in fact, it's quite clear he doesn't realise just how attractive he is.

"You have the best smile, you know that?" I blurt out, like word vomit. Honestly, this lack of sleep thing is affecting my brain. I think even Hendrix is surprised I said it.

"I don't smile often so maybe it's you, Ms Maddison...?"

"Mulligan," I fill in for him.

He takes a step towards me, closing the gap between us.

"Well, Maddison Mulligan, it's been a pleasure."

We pay for our tattoos and step back out onto the street. It's much brighter now with the sun fully in the sky and it has already warmed up to an intense heat, something I'm not sure a British girl like me could ever quite get used to.

"And you are?"

"Caine," he responds. Hendrix Caine – it sounds like a rockstar name. It suits him well.

I check the time, it's almost half past seven now which means the girls will be up soon for their last day exploring Nashville. I need to go back and get my things and have the awkward conversation of telling them I'm choosing to stay behind on my own.

"Here..." Hendrix takes my phone out of my hands and begins typing his phone number into it. "Call me or text me if you run into any problems."

As soon as I take it back, I send a smiley face emoji to his phone.

"There, you have my number too. Just in case." I smile at him reassuringly since he seems worried. I have no idea if he actually is worried, we've only just met, but he does give me that impression.

"What will you do now then?"

"Think I'm going to head back to the ranch. I had planned on staying a day longer but I'm not sure if I can top this night, so may as well quit whilst I'm ahead." He smiles. "What time you going to get the bus to Memphis?"

"Probably by lunchtime, no point in hanging around."

"Well, be safe," he says before awkwardly holding out his hand.

I giggle whilst I shake his hand, wondering how someone this good looking hasn't got more game with the girls than this.

"I will," I reassure him, before pulling my hand away and feeling the reluctance in his fingertips to let go.

CHAPTER TWENTY-FIVE

HENDRIX

"So, you're home already, you're not hungover, you're not still drunk, and you don't look like you've been in a fight. So, you must have joined a cult?!" Tucker fires question after question at me, looking more and more confused.

"One night was enough, what can I say? Plus, I got shit to do." I'm collecting the keys for my lodge today and I'm keen to have my own space and to have something I can call my own. I'm not in Grandma's spare room anymore, or on Tucker's sofa – I'm in my very own home and that has to be a positive step for me. My therapist kept saying that creating my own foundations may give me a sense of belonging, I sure hope she's right.

Tucker scans me up and down suspiciously. "What have you done?"

"Nothing!" I chuckle at his distrust.

"Well if this is your therapist, she deserves a fucking pay rise."

I smile but don't answer, instead I grab the brush ready to sweep away the old hay from the barn.

"Wait! Is that a new tattoo?" Tucker stares down at my hand grasped around the broom.

He's clocked the little cowboy hat that I got for Maddison.

"Uh-huh."

"It's not very you? It's too small and simple for your taste."

Tucker is like a dog with a bone now, staring at me like I'm harbouring some huge secret and not looking like he's going to let it go anytime soon.

"Okay, okay, I'm in a cult, you're right. Our symbol is a little cowboy hat and our mission is to have the cleanest barns in the south. We ride horses, it's crazy and we should be feared."

Tucker looks unimpressed with my sarcasm and a little like he wants to kick me.

"You're an ass!"

"And you're suspicious – can't a guy decide that one night in Nashville was enough and come home unscathed and sober?"

"Sure, some guys can, but you can't."

"Well, maybe I'm finally changing."

Just as I turn my back on him to sweep more hay into a pile, I hear him gasp as if a lightbulb just went off in his head.

"Holy fuck! Did you meet somebody?"

I turn to look at him, but I can't answer. I have met somebody but the chances of me ever seeing her again are slim to none, so it's not like I have anything really to tell.

"You're so sly! Of course you met someone – and you're sober because you probably spent all night with her in your room fornicating like rabbits."

"No, it wasn't like that."

"Of course it was, it's you Hendrix. You're a love 'em and leave 'em kinda guy. I bet you can't even remember her name."

"Maddison, that's her name and that's all you're getting to know." I turn back around and carry on sweeping but somehow I already know Tucker is probably gawping in shock that I remember a name.

"She from Nashville?" He pushes for more information, completely ignoring my warning.

"She's not even from America. But that's it, that's all I'm saying, she's gone now, I probably won't see her again, so I really don't want to keep talking about it."

Tucker nods, accepting the tone in my voice. I actually feel sad saying that out loud. I really don't know if I will see her again, she'll be in Memphis having a great time and eventually I'm sure she'll need to go home and that'll be it.

CHAPTER TWENTY-SIX

MADDISON

"Maddy! Where the hell have you been?" Poppy asks, rubbing her sleepy eyes as she tries her best to focus on me. "We've been worried sick, we thought something awful had happened to you." Her voice is strained and croaky; she does sound like she has been genuinely concerned and it's enough to make me think I should have checked in with her at least to let her know I was safe.

I try not to lock eyes with Hannah, but I see can from the corner of my eye that she's sitting with her arms folded, not looking like she has much to say; if anything, her arms are folded like she's got some attitude.

"I'm sorry Pops, I just needed some space." Her eyes look instantly sad as she realises there is a distance between us that has never been there before.

She gets off the bed as if she is coming to hug me; I step back awkwardly and start picking up my things from the bed and bedside table. "I just came to get my stuff, then I'll be going again."

"Where? Why? Are you going back to England?"

I shake my head. "No, I'm going to spend the rest of my time travelling Tennessee and then I'll go home."

"But we really ought to stick together..." Her voice is thick with concern and worry.

In the corner of my eye, I see Hannah's eyes rolling

dramatically, she obviously wants me to notice. I give in and turn to face her. Her eyes are vacant and cold, she stares at me as if I'm just some annoying girl she met on holiday and not her best friend.

"What?" I snap.

"It's just such a major overreaction, it's not like I slept with your husband, I slept with a man you've grown to hate anyway, so what's the big deal? You just seem to *love* being the victim Maddison, just like Jamie said you would."

Poppy leaps in between us. "Hannah, stop!"

"It's fine, she's already shown me what type of friend she is. It's not like she can make this any worse, we were already over and done with last night."

Hannah doesn't look at all phased by my words; not even an ounce of guilt shows in her expression and she looks completely cold and disconnected from me. It's sad, heart-breaking really, to see what we've become, but in the same breath I'm glad I learned this now rather than waste any more time in a fake friendship. Poppy however looks shattered; the look on her face almost makes me burst into tears but there's no way I'll let Hannah see how hurt I am.

Poppy awkwardly steps closer to me, her head hung in shame. "I'm just so sorry Mads. When Hannah told me about the affair, I told her time and time again to tell you, but then when you and Jamie broke up, I thought maybe it was problem solved. But that was wrong, you should have been told, I should have been a better friend..."

The emotion building up causes her voice to crack and she starts sobbing in front of me. I feel a new pain, grief, but this time not for a relationship I had or the betrayal from Hannah, but at the realisation that I am losing Poppy. She hurt me, but I can understand that she didn't mean to. Her eyes are sad and I know she needs me to reassure her.

I reach my arm out and pull her close to me. Her arms immediately wrap around me, and we hug in silence for a moment.

"I love you Pops; I know you didn't want any of this. I don't blame you, I really don't."

She takes a step back, wiping her eyes on her pyjama sleeve, looking somewhat comforted.

"But I think we all know we can't continue travelling together. If I'm honest, I just need some space to get myself together."

Poppy looks as though she's about to interrupt me with more concerns about my safety travelling alone but I get in quickly to reassure her.

"I'll only be in Memphis for a while and then I'll get on the coach to Florida and meet you at the airport and we can all fly home together. I'll be fine, you'll see."

Poppy gives me another tight cuddle, squeezing me into her as if she doesn't want to let go. When she eventually does, I grab my things and my suitcase and I head out of the door. I don't even say goodbye to Hannah who is too busy texting on her phone anyway to even look up.

I didn't expect to feel sorry for either of them after last night, but now, I feel desperately sad for Poppy. Seeing her so upset hurts me deeply, we've been friends forever and I know that really, she is innocent. She's tried to be the peacekeeper, I get it; she thought she was doing what was best by staying out of it, I can appreciate that. She didn't deserve to be dragged into this.

I awkwardly pull my suitcase along, struggling with my bags and the souvenirs I had already been collecting. The tiredness from the night before is setting in and I'm feeling quite groggy. The humid temperature is suddenly a lot more unforgiving than it was yesterday. I pull out my purse, checking how much cash I have on me before checking the banking app on my phone – it's going to be a struggle without the pre-paid hostel stays I was relying on, but I should be able to make it work for a while. The first thing on my agenda is finding the coach station and booking my ticket for Memphis.

Just as I'm working out which way I should be heading, a message pops up on my screen causing my heart to skip a beat. It's just a row of numbers with no saved name, which makes me realise that it must be Hendrix.

Hey British girl,

Before you leave Nashville and embark on your one-woman adventure, I left you a little something at a store called Ray's near the strip. I'll send the address. Take care, I hope you get to experience the trip you hoped for. Hendrix.

My heart thumps in my chest as I follow the last few steps on Google maps and approach the store. I have no idea what it could be, or why Hendrix wanted to leave me something. I have never been more intrigued in my life – so much so that I practically sprinted here, dragging my suitcase along, which was about as elegant as running with a Henry Hoover.

The store is small and full of gadgets – phones, tablets, computers, telescopes, speakers, all sorts really. A tall man with silver hair and a matching silver beard comes to the counter to greet me; his name badge says Ray. Makes sense.

"How can I be of assistance darlin'?" he says in a thick country accent.

"Um," I shuffle a bit awkwardly. It seems strange to not really know what I am here for.

"A friend left me something here, I think…"

Ray focuses on me. He's half smiling as he watches me awkwardly try to explain while the other half is looking as curious as I am.

"Ah! Wait, yes, you must be Maddison? Of course you are, the accent is a dead giveaway."

I smile with relief that he seems to know what I am talking about.

I nod enthusiastically. "Yep, I'm Maddison."

Ray pulls something up from a cupboard and places it down on the counter.

"For Maddison to collect, the pretty girl I met last night." My cheeks flush red as he reads out the words from the note.

Whatever it is, it's wrapped in brown paper with brown string holding it altogether neatly in a bow, rustic but presentable.

"Would you like a bag?"

"Um," I stare down briefly at the five bags I already have from various other stores. "It's fine, I should be able to fit it in one of these. Do I owe you anything?"

"No, ma'am, it's been paid for in full, it's all yours," he says as he hands me the package. My heart skips again when I feel the weight of the parcel. What could it be?

I give Ray a grateful smile and practically skip out of the store in excitement. I spot a bench nearby and set my bags down and take a seat. I pause for a second, taking in the neat paper one last time. Carefully, I pull the string and untie it from the parcel before running my fingertips along the paper, carefully unsticking the tape.

What the –

"A camera?!"

My gasp is loud and theatrical, embarrassing. I didn't mean to be so loud, I'm sure people on the street are looking over but I can't take my eyes off the sleek, professional-looking camera sitting on my lap. I'm so speechless that even the thoughts in my head aren't sure of what to think first. I have dreamt of a camera like this, but it never felt the right time to splurge on such a thing, especially when Jamie was getting his business up and running. Plus, he would have told me it was a ridiculous amount of money to spend on something that was *just* a hobby.

This is so generous and thoughtful that it has sent chills down my spine. If Hendrix was here right now, I'd tell him that there was no possible way that I could accept such an incredible gift, I know this can't have been cheap. But he isn't here, he left it for me so I wouldn't have a choice but to keep it. Imagine the photos I could take on this – the quality, the sharpness! I can't wait. This is the best gift I have ever received, and he isn't even here to thank.

CHAPTER TWENTY-SEVEN

HENDRIX

"Hendrix, this is stunning." Savannah's jaw drops impressively as she steps inside my new home. "And you got it at such a bargain price!"

"Yeah, well the couple had already relocated so they needed a quick sale."

Tucker sniggers as if I had just cracked a joke. "Yeah... and nothing to do with the realtor you tapped for that extra percent off..." he reminds me smugly. That's one mistake I want to forget, and quickly. Savannah shoots him a glare, so I don't have to. I know she's still sad for Pete, so she won't find any of Tuck's jibes on this funny.

His hands are raised defensively but he manages to laugh it off, softening Savannah's glare.

"Oh come on – it took less than twenty-four hours for Hendrix to fuck up, that's got to be worthy of a joke."

"Not now!" She's firm but gives in to his playfulness. The pair lean into each other and kiss like the happily married couple they are. The smooching sounds force me to roll my eyes and make myself scarce.

I head back to the main bedroom. Just like the rest of the cabin, everything is wooden, even the walls and ceiling; the only exception is a single brick wall at one end of the bedroom which surrounds a fireplace. The whole place has a rustic vibe you don't see much where I'm from. There are two double doors that open onto a balcony, overlooking nothing but fields and trees. The whole place is so different from anything I'm used to yet it feels like it's been made just for me. In all my years, I have never felt like I had a home, until now. This is definitely it; I have finally put down roots and I can really see myself being happy here – well, as happy as I know how to be.

"Wanna hand bringing in all your furniture?" Tuck calls when he finally prises himself away from Savannah.

"No thanks, I'll manage." I don't care how long it takes to do, I just know I really want to do this alone – a few beers, music in the background and my tools. I'm sure this is my equivalent to a woman's candlelit bath – this kind of thing relaxes me.

"Okay, well call us if you need anything."

Once I see Tuck and Savannah pulling out of my gravel driveway, I get to work. First things first, I set up my speakers and link them to my phone then hit shuffle on the country music playlist and crack open a cold beer. My fridge is stocked well, and not with just beer, but all sorts of stuff for lunches and snacks. My therapist would be impressed that I'm using one of those things for more than just chilling my beers.

My mind feels calm and free as I get to work putting flatpack furniture together and arranging my bedroom. It makes sense to start there seeing as I'll need a place to sleep. I don't think of anything else apart from the task in front of me. It's a great feeling, no anger, no sadness, no panic attacks – just building and watching my pad come to life.

The bedroom alone takes me six hours. I stop only to make a pastrami sandwich before admiring my work. The big wooden double bed faces the balcony doors – that was Savannah's suggestion. It was also Savannah's suggestion to buy four bed cushions; despite kicking back on the idea initially, I'm actually pleased she's stubborn and made me buy them. It does look good. A large sage and cream rug lies on the wooden floor, and there's a large slightly reclined cream armchair in the corner between the fireplace and the balcony doors. Two wooden bedside tables with glass lamps sit either side of the bed.

I take a moment to myself and sit on the edge of the cream chair, feeling pleased with what I have managed already. It wouldn't be much to most people, but the sense of achievement I have from something that is so basic is a huge leap in the right direction. A year ago, I was so messed up, I'd just spend my nights drinking until I passed out on the floor; my mind was plagued with so many dark thoughts that I could never have imagined that something like this would bring me a sense of pride. I never thought in a million years that I'd finally be capable of enjoying something like this, but here I am, staring at my bedroom, feeling proud.

I take the last bite of my sandwich, but just before I get up to crack on with the living room, a text comes through on my phone.

Hendrix, I feel awful, I wanted to text sooner but as soon as I got on the coach I was out like a light! Then when I woke up my battery had died, but I made it safely to Memphis, yay!

I wish I had texted sooner to say a huge thank you for my camera. I love it so much. I feel guilty accepting it though. If you've changed your mind about it, you can totally have it back and return it! I would understand. I know it must have been a lot of money, not that I'm asking how much it cost, I just –

A smile spreads across my face, I can feel her awkwardness through my phone, and it makes me laugh. Another message comes through just as I'm reading the last word.

Fuck, sorry, I sent that too quickly. I was rambling anyway. I'm just not used to someone being so generous! Thank you, Hendrix, thanks so much.

My thumb begins typing away instantly, and I ping back a response.

Hey people pleaser, relax. I don't want the camera back, it's a gift, I got it for you, and I wouldn't regret that. Nice to hear you're still awkward in Memphis though. How is it so far? It's moving day for me, in fact let me send you a photo I think you'll appreciate.

I head to the balcony and snap a photo of my view; the sun is setting so the skies are pink, purple and orange, and the sun has lowered behind the trees so that it's only a little visible. I ping the photo straight across to Maddison and sit back down in the armchair whilst I wait for her response. Three dots appear on my screen to show she's replying already. I smile at that, I know she'll be impressed by that photo.

Wow! That view is breath-taking, is that actually from your new home? Where do you live? In a wellness resort!? It's incredible and definitely beats my view.

A photo follows her message, it's a view of a tiny dark room. It doesn't look much better than a prison cell but I'm guessing it's either a basic hostel or a very budget motel that she can afford.

Actually, that particular view is from my bedroom. The living room has panoramic windows, and you can see over the creek, I'll have to show you that tomorrow. Are you okay there? It looks a little… rough around the edges.

Another three dots appear, and she responds straightaway.

It's twenty dollars a night so I can't grumble. I feel pretty safe, apart from the man next door who is keeping me awake by wielding his axe and I'm pretty sure the owner is going to force me to join his cult. Other than that, it truly reflects the half a star it received on TripAdvisor. Oh, and Larry2012 is wrong, the smell of sewage really isn't that sickening.

You're hilarious as aways Miss Mulligan. What's your plans for tomorrow?

Well, as I managed to bring in my accommodation under budget I should still have enough to do some touristy things. Like visit Graceland! Then I'm going to see if anyone would employ me on the low. According to Google I can stay in the US 90 days before it's breaking the law, so that's cool! Well, I have 80 days left, but still. After that though I'm not sure what I'll do, but I don't really want to think about all of that yet. So anyway, tell me about your new home…

The tone at the end makes me feel sad for her. I know she's dreading going home and I know how lost she feels, that is exactly how I had been feeling until I wound up finding this cabin. And now I'm lucky enough to at least feel like I have some place I can call home. I sense she's putting on a brave face and I admire that.

It's out the way of everything, surrounded by trees, land and a creek. It's so quiet that I can't hear much else but the crickets and every star in the sky seems brighter than it ever was back on the east coast. I've managed to finish my bedroom; I was going to get on and do the living room, but I think I'll save it for tomorrow, So, a cold one on the balcony and an early night is probably my plan now. I'll send you more photos tomorrow.

Please do! I can't wait to see them; I'm going to shower and have an early night as well. Thank you for everything, for the night in Nashville, the conversation, the camera… everything.

She ran into me that night, mascara staining her cheeks, eyes puffy from crying, heartbroken after learning her friends had betrayed her, no confidence because of a boyfriend who ridiculed her – and yet I feel like it's me who should be thanking her. I may not have been hurting in the obvious way she was, but my battles have been real and constant. They're still real, still here, but the difference between then and now is that Maddison gave me a glimpse of something I didn't know could be possible. I felt something with her that night that was new, something that gave me hope that there could be a different future for me, one without all the constant anger and fear and grief I have felt. It would be way too much to explain all this to her, as much as I want to let her know that I am just as grateful for her. Instead, I type back *you're welcome* and toss my phone onto the bed.

I grab my cold beer and sit on the balcony, staring out into the darkness, allowing myself to get lost in thoughts of her.

CHAPTER TWENTY-EIGHT

MADDISON

Memphis is a vibrant city with so much going on and so much to see, but I'd be lying to myself if I said I was having a great time. I am in one way, but in another way I feel a little overwhelmed on my own. The crowds are insane the moment I get anywhere close to something touristy and the prices are crazy – it's become clear that because we were part of a large travel group, a lot of our trips were heavily discounted. I paid over a hundred pounds just to see Graceland, which is okay, it's been on my bucket list forever and I am so pleased I did it – it has been preserved impeccably, it is literally like taking a step back in time. But it's all chipping away at my spending money, so much so that I'm not sure how much more touristy stuff I can do and I've only been here for two days.

Thankfully, a few of the museums I wanted to see are a lot cheaper. I've pencilled in a day at the Civil Rights Museum and a few park days at a nature reserve to fill in a few gaps and save some money. I haven't heard anything from Poppy which feels strange, but I hope she's having a good time in Mississippi. It doesn't feel right to be so cut off from them now, but I try not to think about it. I just want to make the best of this trip.

As promised, Hendrix has been sending me photos of his new home and it doesn't disappoint. I'm really happy for him. I only had one night to get to know him, but I know how much he needed this and I feel so excited for him. The photo of the living room is the stuff of dreams, the way the floor length windows continue around half the room, making it so light and showing off the views. I can imagine that it will be really cosy in the autumn when all the trees turn to that burnt orange colour; I bet it'll be beautiful enough for a postcard.

Now and then, Hendrix goes quiet with the texting, and I assume he is busy getting on with everything, but I miss his updates when I don't get them. I don't know whether it's weird to have that feeling so soon or whether it's just because I have bonded with someone who was as lost as I was. Well, *am.*

I fall asleep scrolling through the hundreds of photos I had taken so far on this trip. I skip quickly past the ones with the girls, otherwise I'll tear up, but I take my time looking at the ones from the park that night with Hendrix. There's a few of him in the background, watching me with the most impressive smile; it makes my heart skip a beat, at the time I don't remember being aware of him staring at me, but I definitely did feel the connection we had.

***

The next day I wake up with a spring in my step. I'm headed to the nature reserve for the day and it's completely free. There's supposed to be a lot of wildlife as well as stunning views – it will be the perfect time to really test out my new camera and see what it can do.

I woke up to a few new photos from Hendrix; one was sent just after six in the morning, so he has definitely been busy with the lodge. I still love all the updates.

Last photo, I swear!

Hendrix texts, followed by a photo of his new wooden garden chairs around a fire pit at the front of his lodge. Well, I'd call them garden chairs, but I suppose he'd call them backyard chairs? I don't know, I'm still getting to grips with some of the different words the Americans use. Like yesterday, I went shopping in Walmart for some more supplies and they call a shopping trolley a cart. I like it though – the differences remind me that I'm far away from home and I love that.

I smile at the photo in between sips of my coffee, loving so much that Hendrix has shared so much with me. I'm sitting in an I-HOP, which stands for international house of pancakes where, *apparently,* they do the best pancakes in the world. It feels it would be rude for me not to try some before I head out on a walk around the Misty Trails Nature Reserve.

As a stack of original buttermilk pancakes is set down in front of me, I get my phone out to snap a photo to send back to Hendrix but at the last second, I stop myself. What if Hendrix thinks I shouldn't be eating this stuff, like Jamie used to point out? What if he thinks I *over-indulge*? Eurgh, I hate that I've reminded myself of specific words Jamie used to say. I'm being ridiculous, Hendrix is not Jamie and there is no way he'd say any of that bullshit to me, my brain is buckling under previous attempts to knock my self-esteem and making me overthink. In fact, to prove myself right, I snap a photo of the pancakes with a drooling emoji and send it to Hendrix.

Within minutes a reply comes through.

> *Nice! The ultimate American breakfast I see! Maybe one morning I should try tea and crumpets and we'll have a cultural competition on what's best. PS Take extra water with you, it's supposed to be really humid come midday.*

I smile – not a single mention of carbs or calories, just a fun response on our cultural differences and then a thoughtful pointer to remind me of how humid it gets. Butterflies swarm my stomach: he surprises me. I would never have thought that the tough-looking guy in the bar, covered in tattoos, would be the guy to care about someone like me.

> *Ha-ha. Don't worry, I always take extra water. How's the day going for you?*

> *I know, it's just I remember how quickly I could go from hydrated to feeling like I could pass out when I was Afghan. The heat can really sneak up on you. I'm headed to the ranch in a bit for work. My cousin thinks a couple of the pigs are showing signs of pregnancy so we are going to build a separate pen where they can relax away from the others.*

> *That is so exciting! Well, pigs usually carry for around three months so if he is noticing signs, they must be halfway.*

*To be honest I think setting up a new pen sounds more
exciting than my walk now! Although not as exciting
as taking photos on my new camera will be…*

*Well, whenever the piglets arrive, I'll be sure to send
you photos. I hope you send me some shots later if you
can, can't wait to see all 7500 photos you take.*

*Ha! Just for that I'll take 7501. But seriously, I know I have said
thank you, but thank you again. This really is the best gift ever.*

It's cool. I can't wait to hear about your day.

*I'll message you later tonight and send a few photos.
Have fun building the new pen. Speak soon.*

I read his last message one more time – he can't wait to hear
about *my* day. It stirs up a commotion in my chest, which
seems to happen more and more with him now. I feel like I
need to be somewhat careful though, I can't go falling in too
deep or rushing into anything. I'm very aware that I haven't
long been single and that I've got my own issues to work
through. He is exciting though.

CHAPTER
TWENTY-NINE

HENDRIX

The skies are blue, and the sun is strong, I can feel the heat beating down on my back as I carve out the wood to make fence panels. Tucker strides past me, laughing as he throws on his cowboy hat.

"What's so funny?"

"You're a real redneck now, boy!" he teases with a grin. I hear Savannah giggling from the porch bench; she's nodding and agreeing.

"What the hell does that mean?"

"You've got sunburn on the back of your neck. You are *real* country now whether you like it or not!"

He practically gloats at the fact before jumping on one of the horses and riding away, looking like something from a Clint Eastwood film – yet *I'm* the country boy. I turn to Savannah who just shrugs with a giggle. They used to joke and tease that I'd be chewing tobacco and saying things like *yonder* by the end of the year. I'm not sure what yonder means, and I'm definitely not about to chew tobacco, but I don't think I mind turning a little country. I can see now why Tucker loves it so much – no traffic, no huge crowds of people, nobody is rushing around like crazy, giving themselves a heart attack over their stressful nine to five. Everybody is taking their days at a much slower pace, enjoying the smaller things in life, something I needed to learn and I still am.

Speaking of learning, I have a session with Dr Edwards today.

Suddenly it dawns on me that I should let the family know

that I need to leave early today. "Hey, Savannah, will Tuck be home before four cos I gotta shoot off for my appointment with the head doctor."

She smiles at the head doctor part. "I'm not sure, he went to Deacon's ranch to help him out with something. But don't worry, he wouldn't want you to miss it. Make sure you go."

I nod gratefully. I think they're pleased that I'm finally taking this therapy thing seriously. I'll do anything to stop the blackouts and the dark thoughts, even if it means spilling my guts to a virtual stranger.

I check my phone once or twice when I stop to hydrate and take ten minutes out of the sun, but there's nothing yet from Maddison. I hope she's enjoying her day, God knows she deserves it right now.

"Okay, that's the third time you've checked your phone in twenty minutes."

Savannah has her head tilted to the side, looking me up and down suspiciously. One hand is gently stroking her slightly swollen baby bump. I'm wondering if being a mother is giving her some superpower to read me like a book.

"Second time…"

"Third…" she corrects me. "Come on, I feel fat and tired already, tell me something juicy."

Juicy? I almost cringe. I stare reluctantly at her, but I can't say no to a pregnant woman, especially one who's like a sister.

"Okay… fine, I surrender." She claps gleefully, scooting over on the bench and gesturing for me to come and sit with her.

"I met someone in Nashville…"

"I knew it!" she excitedly interrupts me. "Was she pretty? She must have been. What's her name? Is she from these parts?"

Her questions come firing at me quicker than I can process them, and her smile is from ear to ear as she waits for any information I can give.

"Her name's Maddison. Yeah, she's… she's beautiful. She's not from here though, she's from England."

"British!? Oh my god, I love the British. Does she know Prince Harry?"

Her innocence cracks me up. "Yeah, she lives next door to him."

Her face momentarily lights up before she realises that I am, of course, taking the piss.

"No Savannah, she doesn't know Prince Harry... I don't think."

She listens intently, waiting for me to share more. I can tell she's loving this.

"Before you ask, no we didn't sleep together, it wasn't like that. It was so different, she's so different..."

"I know."

"You know?"

"Sure. I can tell this isn't one of those girls you'd have a one-night stand with."

My eyes narrow. "How can you tell?"

"Because you're different too," she explains carefully. "Your whole demeanour has changed, it's hard to describe. But firstly, nobody keeps checking their phone for a one-night stand and secondly, you look like life isn't beating you down, like you're not so lost."

I pause, thinking about her words, and realise that it makes perfect sense. Because Maddison was the same – she walked into that bar completely lost and scared and when I left her, she was smiling and brave. It's like we helped each other.

"Have you ever felt like you were in the exact right place at the exact right moment? Because that's what it was like that night. Like I was always meant to be in that bar, and she was always meant to find me."

She stares at me, deep in thought, and I notice her eyes fill with tears that she tries to fight back. She blinks quickly and composes herself.

"One night, just before Prom, Tucker turned up at my house early to surprise me with this corsage he'd got from town. He wanted to be sure it matched my dress." She smiles fondly at the memory. "He got to my house just in time to see what my daddy does when he's drunk." Her smile is quick to disappear. "Us kids were always his punching bag; he knew that would hurt my mama the most."

"Oh Savannah, I had no idea..."

"Nobody does, I begged Tucker to never tell a soul and he didn't. But he promised me that from that night on I would be safe and that my daddy would never hurt me again."

"So that's why you went to live with him and my aunt so young?" The penny dropped – I had always wondered why a sixteen-year-old would move in with her high school boyfriend so quickly.

She nods gratefully. "Yep, and then I felt safe enough to report my daddy. He went to prison and my mama and sisters got to live without fear again. If it hadn't been for Tucker that night, then who knows. He was there right when I needed him, he saved me, he saved my whole family."

She pulls out a tissue from her pocket and dabs away the few tears that she was unable to hold back. "God, look at me, I'm a hormonal mess!" she jokes to lighten the moment, but my heart aches at the thought of a young Savannah growing up terrified.

"I know you're not religious Hendrix, but I really believe that God guides us to the people we need. So yes, I do know exactly what you mean by being in the right place at the right time, and if that's how you feel about Maddison then there must be a good reason for it."

I nod. "I think so too."

CHAPTER THIRTY

MADDISON

Twenty-seven photos were all I took on my phone – I can't wait to tell Hendrix and to rub it in that I didn't give in and take my usual seven thousand as he teasingly suggested. Obviously, I'll leave out the part where my phone battery died, which clearly had a big part to play in it. I did, however, take a whole load more on my camera, including one very awesome shot of a blue and yellow butterfly perched on a sunflower with the sun setting behind it. It's the best photo I have ever taken, and I plan to surprise Hendrix with it. Somehow, I'm going to get it put onto a canvas so he can hang it up in his lodge. I haven't worked out the logistics of getting it to him yet, but maybe I can go and visit him in Dayton before I go as a surprise and gift it to him then – as a thank you for the camera of course and not because I'm missing him.

Lying to myself has become my new favourite thing. I'm having a blast in Memphis on my own, I *do not* think about Hendrix *all* the time and I absolutely *have not* wondered what he looks like naked. Those are my top three favourite lies.

It sucks really because I should be having the best time in Memphis, but I think the thing that's holding me back is the uncertainty. I really don't want to go back to England anytime soon. I suppose I could go and spend some time in Ireland and visit my dad. At least it's not England, and I'm sure I could find some work over there for a while. I settle a little bit with that thought, it's something.

"Last stop," the bus driver calls, and I suddenly realise I'm the only one still on the bus and that he must be talking to me.

"Wait, this isn't where I got on!" I look around panicked; it's dark outside now but I don't recognise the street at all.

"This bus goes as far as East Street, where do you need to go?"

Shit, I think, East Street is miles away from where I need to be.

"I'm in a hostel a fifteen-minute walk from Beale Street…"

"Oh honey, it'll take you an hour to walk from here, unless you can find another bus, but most will be stopping for the night now."

I scramble to get my bag and get up off my seat. "Okay, no problem, I'll work something out, thanks anyway." I smile and awkwardly step onto the street with no idea where I'm going or which direction my hostel is in. I can't turn on my phone either for an Uber or to get my maps up because my battery is dead. I tuck it back in my bag with a sigh. The street is quiet, hardly anyone is around; the bus disappears into the depot behind me and leaves me stranded in the darkness.

Maybe if I walk a little bit, I'll end up back by the shops and bars, there's bound to be a tonne of people there who can point me in the right direction. I can't even check the time now but I'm guessing it's getting late. Serves me right for wanting to stay for the sunset. I remind myself of the awesome shot I got – it was worth it, even if I do have to walk an hour to get back to where I'm staying.

"Excuse me miss?" A man's voice startles me. I turn to see a figure in the alleyway; it's dark and I can't really make anything out, just a silhouette of somebody in a hoodie. A feeling of dread washes over me.

"Yes?" I try to sound calm and confident, but I know my answer comes out squeaky.

Within a split second, he leaps towards me and grabs my bag, pulling my shoulder hard. I panic – all the money I have is in this bag. I struggle and try to pull it back, but he is stronger than me. The more I try to keep hold of my bag, the scarier this gets. I know I'm playing with fire, but I can't let go. I scream for help just as I feel a heavy blow to my face. The force of it knocks me off my feet and I lay sprawled out on the concrete sidewalk; everything gets blurry, and I know I've lost the fight for my bag.

CHAPTER THIRTY-ONE

HENDRIX

"So how was Nashville?" Dr Edwards asks in an attempt to sound open-minded, but I reckon she's already assumed that it ended in an arrest.

"Actually, it was really great."

"Oh?" Her voice is pleasantly surprised.

"I started writing stuff down in a journal, it was something my grandma tried to get me to do a lot after my parents died and it actually really helped." I notice Dr Edwards nodding enthusiastically which is a good sign. "Then I ran into this girl…"

She stops nodding so enthusiastically.

"A girl? Like another one-night thing?"

I roll my eyes at the assumption, although it's fair; pretty much the only time I've mentioned women it has involved casual sex.

"No, it wasn't anything like that. She was a lot like me in a way, she was lost and trying to find her feet again. We ended up talking all night long. I think it was the first time I have ever connected with someone like that, you know?"

She scribbles stuff down like she always does and pauses in thought.

"Do you think a relationship would be best for you right now? You're still working through a lot of anger issues and black-outs. I'm not sure it's wise."

"It can't be a relationship; she lives in England."

She looks annoyingly relieved at that information. "But why would a relationship be so bad?"

"I think it would just be *a lot* to handle. We really need to work through what you saw with Martinez if you want to explore an intimate relationship."

"Why?! I didn't rape her!" I snap, allowing my anger to rear its ugly head and annoyingly proving her point that it seems my problems are still hidden beneath the surface, ready to explode. My anger feels warranted though – why the fuck would what Martinez did get in the way of me being serious about a girl?

Dr Edwards relaxes into her chair, allowing me a moment to calm myself down.

"Hendrix, I *know* that Martinez is a rapist. I also *know* that you are not capable of hurting a woman in such a way. But I also know that he was your buddy at the time. I know that it stirred up a lot of emotions and I know you find what you saw hard to deal with. I know you see that girl's face in your blackouts."

And with that, the girl flashes into my mind. Bloodied face, hair stuck to her cheeks from the tears, restrained and scared. "Fuck this," I snap as my chest grows heavy and that breathless feeling comes back. "I'm sorry but I'm not doing this. I'll talk about anything else but not that. I told you this."

I rise to my feet, ready to end the call and go for a walk to cool off, but Dr Edwards persuades me to stay on and assures me we can change the subject, for now.

Eventually, Dr Edwards strikes up a conversation about how I saw my life panning out had my parents not died and what I would say to eight-year-old me if I could go back in time. It was heavy, but I'm learning to deal with that stuff a lot better. I can discuss 9/11, I can be open now about that. But not him, not Martinez. That memory takes me to a dark place, and I don't trust who I become. I lost it that night, I could have killed Martinez, I had no control, and I just don't trust myself.

***

I glance at my watch and realise it's almost six o'clock. I had half expected to have heard from Maddison, but I guess she's still exploring. I need a positive distraction after the gruelling therapy session, but first I decide I deserve a cold beer. I grab that from the fridge, throw a pizza in the oven and put on some Luke Combs in the background. It was Savannah who got me into him, he's not half bad. It's definitely good enough to relax to.

I check my phone a couple more times over dinner but still nothing. It's closer to eight now and dark outside. I type out a quick text message to her in the hope it puts my mind at ease.

Hey, you, looking forward to you blowing me away with these incredible shots! Let me know how it went.

Twenty minutes pass and still no reply. I don't want to be *that* guy who checks the clock every two minutes, but I have this strange feeling that I can't shake. Something doesn't feel quite right. I keep my phone out on the table just in case she calls or texts, but my eyes are growing heavy after the long day in the heat.

I fight to stay awake; I want to know she's alright before I fall asleep. I try to talk myself out of this gut feeling I have and remind myself she could just be out – maybe she made friends and she's partying away, or maybe she went home and fell asleep…

Suddenly I hear screaming, loud high-pitched screams which make the hairs on my arms stand up on end. I run towards the sound and realise that the sand crunching underneath my combat boots is also deafening; everything is so loud and overwhelming that I can barely rationalise my thoughts, but I know I need to follow the scream.

I raise my rifle as I approach some rundown shack. The familiarity of the place casts me with dread. I hear another cry for help just as I kick open the door. Then everything becomes silent. Avery is there, he is smiling in a chilling way as he points to the left of me. I turn to look and that's when I see Martinez. His trousers are dropped to his feet, and he has a sick grin on his face as he restrains a young woman. I dry gulp, struggling to catch my breath, just as the woman turns her face to stare at me. It's Maddison. She looks just like she did in the bar that night – her cheeks are mascara stained, she looks scared and lost and she's begging me to help her, but each time I try to take a step towards her I somehow move further away.

Martinez laughs as he watches my desperation to save her. Her beautiful eyes are pleading for me to rescue her from this monster and yet I'm helpless. Just as Martinez grabs her hair, pulling her up from the table and slamming her hard back onto it, readying himself to violate her, I wake up. Sweat drips down my trembling body. I sit bolt upright, gasping for air. It takes me an uncomfortable amount of time to realise I was dreaming; I don't even remember falling asleep. My eyes whizz around the room, quickly trying to reassure myself of my surroundings: I'm home, deep breath, I'm home.

Some relief washes over me when I come to and realise that I am, of course, in Tennessee, not Afghanistan and Martinez is nowhere near Maddison. It was just a dream, a horrible fucking dream. But as I lean across to grab my phone from the bedside table, I see that Maddison still hasn't responded to my texts. It's almost three in the morning and I'll no doubt look insane, but I need to hear her voice and know she's safe, so I swiftly press the call button, my breath held whilst I wait for it to ring. Nothing. It goes straight to voicemail. I try again, still nothing. The horrible gut feeling I had earlier is now a full-on kick to the stomach. Something isn't right, I feel it.

CHAPTER THIRTY-TWO

MADDISON

I'm still crying when I finally reach the hostel. If it wasn't for the couple who helped me up and got me into an Uber then I'd probably still be lying there. I must have been in shock because I couldn't move a muscle, I just stayed there, still and helpless. The pain from my eye has spread down one side of my face and the constant throbbing is making me feel sick. I just want to get to my room and sort myself out but I'm waiting for another key since mine was in my bag. I've lost everything. My phone, my money, my I.D – everything that was important, gone. Thankfully I still have my passport as that's tucked away in my suitcase but that offers little consolation right now. The hostel assistant can't stop looking at me as she sorts me out another key; she's an elderly woman and she looks unsure as to whether she should say anything. She doesn't in the end, she's probably seen all sorts in the hostel and thought better of questioning me. I haven't seen my face yet but I'm guessing it's bad, it feels horrific.

My legs wobble beneath me as I walk to my room. It all happened so quickly that I had no way of calling for help and even if I could have done, I'm not sure I'd be much use to the police – I have nothing to offer them. I didn't see a single feature apart from a hoodie and that's hardly anything to go on. I'd feel guilty for wasting their time.

I feel physically sick when I catch my reflection in the oval mirror hanging on the wall. The right side of my face is purple and the bruising around my eye has spread down my cheek; the eye itself is severely bloodshot which would explain why I'm still suffering from double vision and can barely see out of it; my whole cheekbone is swollen and puffy. It's actually scary to look at it, I don't even look like myself.

I collapse onto my bed and sob. My phone charger is poking out of the socket right next to my bed where I left it, which just makes me cry harder. I wish I had my phone more than ever right now. Who could I call though? My mum? God, that would be a terrible idea; she already feared this trip wasn't safe enough, I'd hate to have to listen to an hour of *I told you so's* followed by her demanding I get a plane home by the morning. I could call Poppy but she's hours away now.
There's one person I do wish I could call though, one person who would definitely want to help me, and that's Hendrix. I knew from the moment I met him that he had a fiercely protective nature about him and that only became more evident when he walked in front of me to shield me from all the drunks that night. Even though I'm sure they were harmless, he clearly wasn't someone who was going to risk it.

With that thought, I'm on the floor and searching every section of my suitcase, every zip-up compartment in my bag and every pocket of my clothes. I know I put cash somewhere else, I must have done. A huge sigh of relief rises from my chest as I find a fifty dollar note in a pair of shorts that I wore on my first day here. It's not a lot, but it's something.

I ponder whether I should go to Dayton, but I worry that it's far too desperate and crazy. I wanted to find jobs that were cash in hand and be able to stand on my own two feet not rely on Hendrix. The poor guy might just end up with far more than he bargained for.

I toss the idea back and forth in my head, but it doesn't change the fact that I am already frantically packing with every intention of getting on a coach first thing tomorrow. I need him – I need a friend, I need a break. I need to feel safe because, quite frankly, this could be the most scared I have ever been in my life. This wasn't how I imagined this trip would be, even on my own. I thought I'd manage just fine and yet here I am – my head is pounding, my eye is so painful I feel physically sick and I can barely focus on much around me. It's terrifying. I'm trying not to let the fear get a hold of me but it's a battle I'm already losing.

Once I'm packed, I lay on the unmade single bed, tucking my legs up against my chest and cradling them in an attempt to comfort myself. The more I cry the more my eye stings. I try to hold my emotions back to minimise the pain. I rock myself gently, praying that I'll just fall asleep. I have that horrible shakiness in my chest, a bit like when a child has a tantrum and then can't catch their breath after. I keep my eyes closed and continue rocking myself, hoping and praying that the pain stops long enough that I can drift off.

CHAPTER THIRTY-THREE

HENDRIX

I jump out of the truck and head straight to the barn where I expect to find Tucker. I'm relieved he's there because then I haven't got to waste time searching for him.

"I'm off to Memphis, I'll be back when I can," I say firmly before heading back to the truck.

"Woah, wait, hold up! Memphis, why?"

I'm aggravated that he expects me to stop and explain when I'm quite clearly in a rush to hit the road.

"Hendrix, wait up. Memphis is six hours away. What's going on?"

As I hop back into the truck, I see a confused Savannah rushing out from the house, gesturing for me to wait.

"Fuck," I sigh heavily which makes Tucker look more confused, staring between me and Savannah for an answer. I reluctantly wait for her.

"What's going on? Is it Maddison?" she calls, out of breath.

I nod and glance at Tucker who is slowly connecting the dots.

"Has something happened?"

"I don't know." I climb back out of the truck and start pacing, my hands rubbing my neck impatiently. "She was going to message me last night when she got back to wherever she's staying but she hasn't."

"Okay. So, her battery could have died? She could have just been tired and forgot?"

I shake my head irritably. "No, something's wrong, I can feel it."

I notice Tucker smirking at my dramatics as if this is all a skit. "Wow, this is hilarious Hendrix – when did you get so whipped?"

I dart towards him, teeth clenched, before I realise what I'm doing and take a step back.

"Tucker, go inside and fix me some tea please. Come on, let me talk to him, you're not helping."

Tucker's face drops when he realises I'm not in the mood for kidding around. He shrugs off my angry lunge and heads back towards the house. I carry on anxiously pacing, stressed to fuck and just wanting to hit the road already.

"Hendrix, just take a moment."

I look back at the truck, wanting desperately to just be in it and making my way to her.

"Hendrix, look at me, look at me Hendrix…"

I give in and my eyes meet her sympathetic stare.

"Talk me through it. What's got you thinking this way?"

"I had this dream last night, I don't want to go into it, but it left me with this feeling that something isn't right. I can't shake this feeling that it may be a sign, maybe something is wrong. She could be in danger, and I'm just fucking stood here doing nothing. She might need me…"

Savannah nods intently. "Sounds like it was a horrendous dream, but that's all it was."

"No, it can't be because I have this weird gut feeling…"

"Hendrix, you were in the Marines so long it's normal to think the worst, it's normal to think you've got to protect everybody that you care about, but I promise, nothing you've said sounds like there's trouble. Why don't we wait and see if she texts back by tonight before you go rocking up to Memphis. You don't want to come off too intense, right?"

I'm hesitant but I know that since the Marines I don't always think rationally. I don't want to rush to Memphis and see she's just been busy – Savannah is right, I'll look like some crazy stalker.

"You sure I shouldn't be freaking out like this?"

"I'm sure… Let's give it a little more time and if you hear nothing then I'll even come with you."

I'm very hesitant. I'm battling against my instincts, but I trust Savannah and I know she's usually the voice of reason.

I squeeze my eyes shut, trying to push away the dark thoughts that keep clouding my judgement.

"She's nowhere near Martinez," I say with a slow exhale.

I realise what I just muttered, and I didn't mean to. Savannah looks up but she pretends that she didn't really catch what I said, instead, she gives my arm a little comforting squeeze and heads back into the house.

CHAPTER THIRTY-FOUR

MADDISON

"The next bus leaves at three o'clock and that'll be thirty-eight dollars and fifty cents."

My heart drops. "Nothing earlier at all?"

"Nothing that'll get you to Dayton, no. Do you want the ticket or not?"

I nod and hand over my forty dollars. I had to use five dollars to pay for the key I lost and another couple of dollars buying myself some water. I'm now officially skint; I have no money and no means of communication. To say I feel completely stressed out would be an understatement.

"Sorry, how long is it to Dayton?" I ask the already restless receptionist.

"It's a six-hour trip ma'am, you're scheduled to arrive at nine o'clock tonight."

"Okay, thank you."

I take my ticket and walk towards a bench to sit for a moment, not really sure what to do with myself – it's barely ten in the morning, it's going to be a long time to wait until three. I notice lots of people staring at me, well they're probably staring at my eye which is worse than last night since the swelling has doubled. My vision is still awful, and the pain is throbbing so bad that I threw up this morning, not the best way to start my day.

"Ma'am?" the restless receptionist surprises me by standing next to the bench.

"Oh? Yeah?"

She hands me a little pamphlet that she's folded up discreetly. Confused, I open it carefully and see straight away it's a help number for a domestic abuse charity. I feel awful that she's made this assumption but before I have the chance to reassure her, she walks away. I feel quite moved that a stranger would reach out like this to help; obviously I'm not experiencing abuse, but her thoughtfulness is heart-warming. It makes me wonder how many women regularly pass through here, fleeing toxic relationships. Reminds me of a Nicholas Sparks movie I watched where a young girl disappeared on a coach, moved somewhere far away from her abusive boyfriend and ended up with a new life and Josh Duhamel. Well, not actual Josh Duhamel as he was just the actor, but you get my point, it was a good movie. And Josh Duhamel is hot.

The next few hours go painfully slowly and I'm desperately trying to savour every drop of my water, but the heat is making it hard.

Eventually, the bus pulls in half an hour before three which means I can at least get comfortable in my seat and maybe even try to sleep.
"Oh Jesus darlin', that's a shiner if I ever did see one." The driver gawps at me as I clamber onto the bus.

I smile and nod but I'm so tired now and in so much pain it hurts to even open my mouth, so I quietly get to my seat and pray he isn't going to ask about it.

Somehow, the next thing I know I'm waking up with the rain battering hard against the window. It's dark outside and I can't make much out, but there's no bright lights and tall buildings anymore so I know we are far from the city now. We pull into the services for a quick pit stop and I use it to go to the toilet and try to freshen up a little bit. It's suddenly dawned on me that I'll hopefully be seeing Hendrix soon and I look awful. I run my fingers through my long hair – it's gone naturally wavy which I don't mind but my face is pale and so puffy still. I don't think any concealer would hide this, and I shudder at the thought of applying it anyway, the pain would not be worth it. It's getting a little chilly from the storm so I chuck on my grey hoodie, which is nice and cosy and makes me feel safer.

Once I'm back in my seat, the bus driver informs all the passengers that we have just under two hours left of the journey. I feel a sense of relief, like everything might be okay soon. I just need a day or two to get myself sorted. Hopefully Hendrix will let me crash on his sofa which should give me just enough time to call my bank, get a new phone and find somewhere cheap to stay for the rest of my trip. I'm sure once my eye looks less scary to customers, I could find a job waitressing or in a bar.

The rain seems to ease up the closer we get to Dayton which I'm grateful for – I didn't fancy looking like a drowned rat on top of everything else. Every time I glance at the red digital clock on the coach, my heart starts beating quicker. I'm so nervous that I will look insane for doing this but deep down I think Hendrix will be happy that I came to him instead of struggling on my own. At least that's what I keep telling myself.

More and more people start getting off at stops along the way and eventually I'm the only one left. I decide to move to the front seat so that the driver doesn't forget I'm here.

"So not many people go all the way to Dayton, huh?"

"No ma'am, there's not a lot in Dayton, I usually have an empty bus before then. You live there?"

I shake my head. "No, just visiting a friend."

"Well, you can let your friend know you'll be there in twenty minutes."

Twenty minutes? Shit. Twenty minutes! Now my heart really is beating fast. What if he isn't home? What if he thinks I'm some stalker? Oh Jesus, what if he's married?! I mean, I definitely don't think he is married because that is absolutely not the vibe that I got from him, but you never know, you see it all the time in soap operas back home. Chill, Maddison, this isn't *Eastenders*.

I drink the last of the warm water from my plastic bottle, which is definitely not as refreshing as it was six hours ago. Out of the windows it's all pitch black – it doesn't at all feel like we are approaching a town. I can't make anything out but I'm assuming it's all fields out there. God, it reminds me a little bit of that *Jeepers Creepers* movie, you know, where the school bus is driving at night in the middle of nowhere and they get stranded... or *Texas Chainsaw Massacre*. I stop my thoughts. Good one Mads, think of every horror movie you've ever seen before you get off the coach, that's a smart move.

"Okay, we're here."

"This is it?" We've pulled into a tiny town with a few dim streetlights that light it up just enough for me to make out how small it is. It's just a strip, at the top is a bar and then side by side is a row of stores and businesses, but not loads. I can see the end of the strip from the coach.

"Yep, told you there's not much in Dayton. You want me to wait for your friend to arrive?"

"Oh no, it's fine," I answer awkwardly. "They're on their way," I lie.

I step off the coach with my suitcase. The door shuts behind me making me jump and within seconds the coach pulls away leaving nothing but a cloud of dust in its tracks.

Oh fuck, what do I do now? Where are all the houses?

My eye is still blurry but if I squint, I think I can make out lights from the bar. Thankfully it looks open and someone in there must know Hendrix and where I might find him. I drag my suitcase through the gravel and hurry quickly to the bar; relief settles over me when I hear music and voices.

As soon as I walk inside everybody stops talking and turns to stare at me. And I don't get the feeling it's because of the huge black eye but rather that I'm a stranger to this town. There's definitely a sense of a tight-knit community here, where everybody knows everybody, you can feel it instantly.

"Lord Jesus, ma'am, are you okay?" the bartender asks me in the thickest southern accent I have ever heard.

I realise now that he is staring horrified at my eye.

"Oh yeah, I'm okay, this was an accident but I'm here looking for someone, I'm hoping you can help?" I step closer to the bar hoping to have a more private conversation without everybody staring.

"Sure, who are you looking for?"

"Hendrix Caine? He's fairly new here himself."

"What does a pretty thing like you want with that asshole?" a man from across the bar pipes up.

"Calm down Pete, it's not our business."

My face burns with social anxiety. I feel like all eyes are fixed on me even more now that I've mentioned the name Hendrix. I guess not everybody finds him as kind as I did...

"I heard Hendrix just bought the lodge next to the creek," the bartender continues.

"Ah okay, so is there a door number? Is it on like a cul-de-sac or something?"

An echo of sniggering and whispers ripples around me, making me realise I must have said something stupid.

"Darlin', you're in the country now. Hardly anyone here lives next to each other. The creek is about a mile up the dirt road behind the bar, but it's not well lit. You got a flashlight on your phone?"

"I, er, I lost my phone," I answer.

"I'll give you a lift, come on, my truck's out front."

It's Pete who offers which surprises me considering he just called Hendrix an asshole.

"But…"

"But nothing, I may not like the guy, but I can't have a young girl getting lost in the dark."

The bartender smiles and nobody objects, so I feel some security that Pete must be a decent guy who can be trusted. It's still a scary thought though, to get into a truck with a stranger, I wouldn't dream of doing it back home. But with no better offer, I thank the bartender and follow Pete to the truck. He takes my suitcase for me and places it in the backseat.

"Hop in," he says cheerily as he opens the door for me.

I do as I'm told and try desperately to ignore yet more horror films that spring to mind. What the hell am I doing?

CHAPTER THIRTY-FIVE

HENDRIX

Savannah hands me and Tucker a second cold beer from the fridge and takes a seat next to us. The fire is roaring and the crackling noises are relaxing, but I can't settle knowing that Maddison still hasn't made contact.

The crickets are filling in the complete silence that we'd otherwise be in. Savannah and Tucker both know I'm on the edge of losing my cool and it's made the evening awkward to say the least. I still have this horrible gut feeling that something is off. I've tried my hardest to ignore these feelings – like Savannah said, I'm programmed to think worst case scenario, it's all I knew in Afghanistan – but I'm kicking myself now that I didn't trust my instincts and just go to Memphis.

"So, nothing at all huh?" Tucker asks, finally breaking the silence before swigging at his Budweiser.

Savannah keeps glancing at me guiltily through the flames of the fire. She chews her bottom lip, contemplating whether she should say anything.

I don't answer Tucker, just shake my head and throw back my beer.

Savannah is next to break the silence. "Hendrix, I'm so sorry…"

"No, don't apologise, you were coming from a good place, you always are."

She nods but I can tell she still feels the weight of telling me not to go looking for Maddison. It's not her fault – I'm a stubborn ass and if I'd wanted to go, I would have, but I also knew Savannah could be right, she still might be. It's hard to think clearly when a background of war reminds me that the world can be an ugly place.

"Look, I don't want to be the bad guy here but maybe she just wasn't that interested?" Tucker's suggestion immediately fucks me off but mostly because it feels too disappointing to even think about; it can't be that – I was there, I felt a connection, it was different.

"Fuck you, Tucker," I snap before downing the rest of my beer and hoping it drowns the anxieties with it.

"Woah! I was only saying, you don't have to lose your head all the time. I was about to ask how therapy is going but I don't think I need to…"

Savannah nervously interjects. "Tucker…"

His tone softens and he slouches back into his chair with a sigh. "I don't mean to be an ass, but maybe it's just one of those things, maybe it wasn't meant to be anything more than what it was."

I don't answer, just keep staring into the bright orange glow of the fire and thinking of Maddison. At this point, I don't even care if Tucker's right, I just wish I knew if she was safe or not, anything to stop this worry I feel.

"Hey, why don't we play cards?"

"You're rubbish at cards!" Tucker teases his sweet wife, but she isn't slightly offended, instead she playfully punches his arm.

"Just for that you can go and get the cards!"

Before I can disappoint them both by telling them that I don't even have cards, I hear a car pulling up next to the lodge.

Tucker curiously arches his neck to try and look around the tree that's blocking the view.

"That's Pete's truck."

Savannah looks panicked, automatically eyeing me up. "Oh god, what did you do now?"

I shrug. "I've done nothing, I've been working my ass off here."

I hear a car door open, followed by footsteps on the gravel and sure enough Pete calls my name.

"Don't worry Marine boy, I'm not here for trouble, I'm helping the little lady get to you in one piece."

What little lady?

I lean forward in my chair; I can see Pete now with help from the glow of the fire and a familiar figure step out from behind him, pulling a suitcase. Her demeanour is timid and vulnerable but as she steps forward my heart beats hard against my chest.

"Maddison!?"

She nods before I catch her bottom lip quivering. I study her face which knocks me back a step – it's purple and bruised, one eye almost completely closed from swelling, and she looks so dejected and lost. A far cry from the girl I left in Nashville. My eyes darken as I take it all in, feeling completely sick that something awful *has* happened. I knew it, I fucking knew it.

I lunge towards her, cupping her face immediately in my hands, studying every inch of her injuries. The adrenaline rushes through my body as every worst-case scenario plagues my mind.

I can't speak, I just keep staring, feeling her pain and thanking all the stars in the sky that whatever happened she still made it here to me.

"Well, my job is done," Pete announces before heading back to his truck. I give him a grateful nod which he reciprocates before leaving.

My eyes focus straight back to Maddison who seems to tremble beneath my hands.

"Who the *fuck* did this to you, Maddison? Was it that Jamie? I'll kill him…"

She shakes her head, sobbing. "No, it wasn't Jamie, I was attacked in Memphis, and they stole everything, my bag, my phone, my money, even your camera…"

"And they did this to you? Just for a fucking bag?"

"It's my fault really, I tried to fight him off and he hit me."

My jaw clenches and I grit my teeth tightly at the thought, my temper flaring at the image of some scumbag putting his hands on her.

I pull her into my arms and she buries her face in my chest as she cries softly; my hand reaches up to the back of her head, comforting her as much as I can.

"I got you." I whisper.

Savannah and Tucker get up quietly from their chairs and mouth goodbye as they decide it's best to leave me to it. I'm grateful, I don't want Maddison overwhelmed by more people than she needs right now.

"Come on, let's get you inside." I take her suitcase in one hand and take her hand in the other; she grips me tightly, I know she's needed me.

She's barely a foot inside the lodge when she turns to me awkwardly. "Hendrix, if this is too weird, I can find a motel, I think I saw one six miles back..."

"Don't be silly," I cut her off quickly. "I'm happy you're here."

If I'm honest, I don't think I'd relax if she was anywhere else but here, I need to take care of her.

I lead her to my corner sofa under the large panoramic windows and get her seated. Just as she eases onto the couch she gasps in pain.

"What is it?!"

"It's just my eye and my head, I keep getting these shooting pains every now and again and then it's just a constant ache."

"Okay, let me take a look..." Gently, I guide her head back into the cushion and tilt her face to assess her injuries. I don't have a medical degree, but I saw enough in Afghanistan to recognise a few things.

Carefully, I swipe her hair away from her face and tuck it gently behind her ear. My heart sinks for her as I take it all in – it's severe.

"Okay, I think it's a fractured eye socket – we should probably take you to the emergency room."

But her head shakes straight away at the thought. "No, I can't, I'm so drained right now. Please Hendrix, can we stay here? I'll see how it goes first."

My face frowns momentarily at her stubbornness but I know I'm not about to argue. "How about you rest, and I take you to the town's doctor in the morning?" She reluctantly nods, meeting me halfway.

Her head rests back on the cushion and her eyes softly close, no doubt relieving her from the pain and discomfort.

"Okay, well first things first, let me dim the lights in here, the brightness won't be helping the pain."

She nods slightly which tells me she's absolutely exhausted

from the last twenty-four hours. I'm comforted though at how relaxed she seems here, with me.

Once I have turned all the lights off apart from one dim lamp in the corner, I make her a hot drink – thanks to Savannah's new home hamper, I have hot chocolate. I make us both one and bring it to her on the couch.

"Are you hungry? I can fix you a sandwich?"

"Oh no, I'm fine honestly." I get the sense she's just being polite, but I don't push her.

Her eyes light up at the mug of hot chocolate which gives me a sense of warmth that I have done something to make this night a little better for her. Inside me, the urge to take care of her grows. I don't know if this is a normal feeling because I have never felt it before, but this need to make her happy is only getting stronger.

"I have a cold pack in the freezer, it'll help with the swelling." I offer and she doesn't protest on this one. As I place it carefully over her eye, she winces for a second but then relaxes into it.

The thought of Maddison being hurt brings the threat of a black-out all too close; inside, my emotions are trying to get the best of me. I could so easily let my anger spill over and smash my fist into a wall or, better yet, get into my truck and drive to Memphis looking for the fucking scumbag who attacks innocent women. For the first time though, I realise that I am managing to conceal it well – it's not easy, but I know she needs *this* side of me, not hot-head Marine Hendrix, she doesn't need him right now. And I'll be whoever she needs to feel better. I'm doing it for her.

CHAPTER THIRTY-SIX

MADDISON

Little goosebumps rise from my skin at every touch, from tucking my hair behind my ear to gently applying the compress to my face, every touch is so gentle but electric. There is definitely a spark between us – I felt it in Nashville, and I know I can't be imagining it.

He is being so kind and so comforting, just like I knew he would be. I relax quickly around him, even if I am a little embarrassed that I cried when I saw him. I have no idea where those tears came from, I just had this sudden rush of relief and all my emotions bubbled over. I don't think I realised how scared I was until I felt safe again.

Hendrix takes a seat on the light brown sofa next to me; he's wearing dark blue jeans and a fitted white t-shirt which shows off every curve and muscle in his upper arms. He looks seriously good right now – and I look like an extra in a disaster movie.

He stares at my bruised and swollen eye, deep in thought.

"What?"

He sighs irritably into both his hands. "This wouldn't have happened if I was with you, I'd have kept you safe, you know that don't you?"

I nod. "Of course, you're a Marine, it's what you do."

"No." He shakes his head. "Not because I was in the Marines...

because it's you."

My heart pounds against my chest – to hear him confirm that there really is something between us makes me feel all tingly.

"We've just met…"

"Yeah, and you feel it too, don't you?" he asks with so much confidence that I doubt whether it's even a question anymore.

I ponder for a second, making sure to answer him truthfully. "All I know is that I have thought about you a lot since we met and when I was attacked, you were the one I knew I needed…"

He closes the small gap between us as he leans forward and presses his lips hungrily against mine, like he'd been waiting to do this since the second I got out of Pete's truck. Tingles shoot through my body, causing every inch of me to feel sensitive. It takes me completely by surprise but I'm not complaining. His mouth is warm and inviting, I part my lips slightly, hoping that he'll slide his tongue against mine and instantly he does, just as I hope. He is gentle though, his hand comes up and carefully cups my cheek, so tenderly and slowly, careful not to cause me anymore discomfort. I kiss him back, growing more passionate and breathless as my heart quickens with excitement. I feel his arm wrap around my waist and pull me closer to his body. The passion between us is electric, but almost as quickly as it started, Hendrix pulls away, catching his own breath and composing himself.

"I want to, so bad, the old Hendrix… Actually, that's not important, the point is, I have these feelings for you Maddison, but I know this needs to be taken slow. You need your rest first."

I try and slow my breathing. I'm disappointed but I know I should be pleased that he slowed this down – my whole life is up in the air right now, I'm running on empty and I'm in need of a good night's sleep.

"Let's get you to bed, I'll take the couch."

It's impressive how well he regains control of himself.

"Don't be silly, I'll take the couch. Or we can share the bed?" I suggest, suddenly realising I sound like I'm insinuating that I'm pushing for sex, and I blush when I hear how I sound.

He smirks. "I don't think I could trust myself!"

I smile in agreement before taking another sip of my hot chocolate. Sex is something I have never rushed into in the past, but here with Hendrix, I really don't trust myself either.

"I know you're in pain and I know you're exhausted; I can hold off until the time is right. I just know I like you too much to fuck anything up..."

He's not wrong – I am in pain and exhausted – and really, I love so much that he is such a gentleman about this. But if that was a small taster of what's to come then the idea of there being a next time makes me buckle at the thought. That was one of the best kisses I have ever had, he took his time, savouring every taste of me; nobody has ever touched me like that, nobody has made me feel so needed and so wanted.

"I like you too, Hendrix." I smile, pleased we've said it out loud.

Like the gentleman he is, he takes my suitcase and carries it down the hall to his bedroom. I follow on behind, anxiously pulling at my sleeves. When I step inside, he's already plumping up the pillows and folding back the duvet, my heart melts at his thoughtfulness.

"You should sleep with your head as propped up as possible, that'll take some of the pressure off."

"Thank you..."

"Do you have clean clothes to change into or do you want to wear one of my t-shirts to bed?"

I still have one pair of clean pyjamas that I haven't yet worn but I'll keep that to myself, his t-shirt sounds way more appealing.

"No, I don't think I have…"

He smiles as if he is just happy to help and heads over to his wardrobe and grabs a black t-shirt with a white print of an American eagle on the back.

"Here, this is soft enough, should be comfortable to sleep in."

"Thank you… not just for the shirt, but for being, well, you."

He smiles again but this time it's bigger, showing off his perfectly straight teeth.

I gaze around the room, impressed at the simple yet cosy décor.

"Wait 'til you see the view in the morning, it's my favourite."

The *view* – it reminds me of that incredible shot I got on my camera just for Hendrix and now I can't show him.

I slump down on the edge of the bed, bringing my hands to my head. I can't believe I lost that shot. It would have gone perfectly in his lodge.

"Hey? What's wrong?" He appears at the edge of the bed, standing in front of me and carefully pulling my hands from my face.

"The camera… I had this incredible photograph; it had the sun setting behind it. I waited until the very end to get it, I had planned to put it on a canvas print for you, it was going to be a thank you for the gift. But that camera has probably already been sold on and the photo long gone."

"Maddison…" He lowers himself until we are at eye level. "The fact that you've been through so much and yet you got on a bus with the last of your money, travelled across Tennessee, walked into a bar with a bunch of sheltered locals to look for me and even got into a truck with a stranger just to try and be here, with me – that's the best fucking gift of all."

This time, it's me that makes the lunge towards him. I take both my hands and wrap them around his neck, kissing him emotionally, soaking him up. He doesn't stop it, he leans forward, pushing me carefully back onto the bed, using his hand to steady me. He climbs on top, keeping his mouth against mine, I take pleasure in feeling the weight of him. I feel so protected under his huge broad shoulders that I let out a relieved cry, prompting him to stop and stare at me instead.

"Maddy?"

"I'm just happy," I say catching my breath. "You make me feel so safe."

CHAPTER THIRTY-SEVEN

MADDISON

It takes me several seconds to remember whose bed I'm in when I open my eyes; these new surroundings are comforting compared to the last hostel. The rays from the sun are drifting beautifully in through the windows, making the bed a sun trap. I quite like the warmth against my skin, it makes me want to lay here longer, but I'm curious to see if Hendrix is still asleep on the sofa.

True to his word, we didn't let it go too far last night – we kissed a lot and cuddled, he took care of me in a way nobody has before, he held me. I have never been held before, it was like he was bringing me to safety by holding me close to his body and wrapping his arms around me, protecting me and shielding me from the world.

The last thing I remember was falling asleep just like that, my head against his chest, as he whispered that he'd only be next door on the couch if I needed him. I wanted him to stay, I wanted to go off into a deep sleep in his arms, but I was too tired to protest. I let him go, knowing he was being the gentleman I met back in Nashville.

I tiptoe across the wooden floor and make my way to the door, opening it as quietly as I possibly can, then tiptoe down the hallway to the lounge. I see straight away that the blanket has been folded up and placed on the end of the couch with the pillow – Hendrix isn't here. Just as I go to look for him on the porch, I spot a note on the coffee table.

Morning, I didn't want to wake you. I had to go to the ranch to help Tuck finish the pen before the pigs go into labour. I'll be home at lunch, and we can drop by the doctor's office. Rest up. P.S I left you breakfast on the side.

I curiously peer over my shoulder and see on the kitchen side what looks like a bowl of oatmeal with a plastic lid popped on top. Did he wake up early to make me this? The evidence suggests that he did, and it makes my stomach swarm with butterflies. Saying that, my stomach now growls with hunger – I haven't eaten in over twenty-four hours and that oatmeal looks heaven sent. I warm it up in the microwave, stir in some maple syrup that was left next to it and head onto the porch. It's a beautiful day, and while the porch is quite shaded by all the trees, the sun still manages to bleed through, warming my forehead and cheeks in the process. It's so quiet and pretty with all the landscape and nature surrounding it; I can even hear water trickling in the creek behind. I'm trying to picture which movies this place reminds me of, maybe *Hannah Montana* when she heads back to her roots, or even a scene from *Steel Magnolias*. Something along those lines anyway, but in person, a view like this is better than any movie.

***

I'm sitting in a quaint little waiting room; it doesn't look like it has been updated much since the seventies but it's not shabby, it actually looks charming. There are only two doctors in this town and one of them is on maternity leave; that thought makes me smile – one doctor to a whole town, it really is like taking a step back in time, but in a comforting kind of way, there's a real personal touch here. I watch on, reassured that this doctor clearly cares a great deal about his patients; he talks about them to the receptionist with ease, like he can remember everybody's medical history just by hearing their first name.

Hendrix interrupts my thoughts by reaching out and placing his hand on my thigh; it's comforting and calming. I'm not particularly nervous about seeing the doctor, but I am nervous about the cost. I have no bank card still and I can't even remember if I took out health insurance – I think I automatically had some cover when I booked with the travel group, but I'm no longer with them, I'm completely solo, so I'm probably not covered by the insurance and I dread to think what the charges are going to be.

"Ms Mulligan." The doctor calls my name with a bright friendly smile. He gestures towards his office door and Hendrix follows closely behind.

I'm laid up on the grey leather medical bed and the doctor, who I now know is called Doctor Garett, is shining a flashlight across my eye. He makes me follow his finger and studies my eyes carefully before taking my blood pressure and pulse.

"Okay," he announces, sounding sure of what he has observed. "It's definitely a fractured eye-socket, which should heal on its own, but it'll take time. You'll need antibiotics to reduce the chance of infection and you'll need some eyedrops. Your blood pressure is a little high, but I'm not too concerned considering you're probably still in shock after the attack. You will need to take it easy for a while and use ice packs regularly to reduce the swelling."

Shit – antibiotics would cost enough on their own, but eyedrops too. This could be a hundred dollars already and I have nothing, I can't ask Hendrix for help, he has done enough already, letting me bombard his space; he needed his own space more than anything and I've turned up like a bull in a China shop.

"Don't worry about the antibiotics, it should be fine…" I blurt as I gather myself up off the bed and get ready to leave.

The doctor looks incredibly confused as to why I'd refuse treatment but not as confused as Hendrix.

"What? Maddison? If it's the money, I'm happy to pay…"

"No! You've done so much; I'm not going to ask more from you…"

"Don't be silly, it's just some antibiotics, you need them, and I *want* to…"

The doctor watches us back and forth as Hendrix insists and I refuse. You'd think the poor bloke was at a Wimbledon match the way his head darts between us both.

"Actually… neither of you will be paying today."

Before I have a chance to protest to the doctor, who is surely just trying to be kind, he says something that makes me instantly emotional.

"That little girl you pulled from the school fire just happened to be my granddaughter, so please, both of you, take the antibiotics without charge and enjoy the rest of your day. I insist. You're a hero, Hendrix."

Hendrix tenses up beside me and his eyes drop to the floor; he mumbles a quick thanks and marches out of the office with an attitude that wasn't there moments ago.

"A school was on fire, and you went in?" I ask Hendrix as soon as we are back outside and on the street.

"It was nothing, most people would have done the same."

"No, most people wouldn't have done the same, they'd have called the fire department and waited. What you did was so selfless, you did something incredible… you're that guy's hero."

"Enough!" he snaps before realising what he did and looks even more irritated at himself. "Just please stop, I'm not a hero. Okay? I'm just not."

His pace picks up as he heads to the truck, and I find myself practically jogging behind to keep up.

"Hendrix, wait, what's so wrong with being called a hero?"

"Just get in the truck…"

"But…"

"Dammit Maddison, will you stop asking me a million questions all of the time and just get in the damn truck."

I do as I'm told but I immediately feel myself withdrawing from him just as much as I am from this conversation. He switched so quickly – the doctor did nothing but thank him and now he's furious and on edge. I look at him briefly in the truck; his dark brown eyes are focused on the road, he has one hand on the steering wheel and the other hand is supporting his head as he rubs at his temple.

Perhaps this is my cue to leave, because really, what do we know about each other? One night can't tell me everything I need to know. As much as I wanted to get carried away in this fairy tale and soak up every inch of Hendrix Caine, I realise how naïve I have been. In my head, I felt like Hendrix could be my answer to everything, I thought he could be the best thing to come out of this trip – but what if I'm wrong?

CHAPTER THIRTY-EIGHT

HENDRIX

I can't even bring myself to look at her. She's been through so much and then I go and snap at her like the asshole I am. I just snapped; I don't want to feel triggered every time I hear the word *hero* but it's not easy. In this instance it just made me feel overwhelmed, like if she looks at me as if I'm some kind of hero I'll just end up letting her down, like I felt let down by my own dad. I wince at how painfully cruel that sounds, but my therapist reminds me that resentment is a very normal response in grief.

I'm barely in the driveway when she opens the truck door and darts out of it like she's on a mission. She's going to leave me, I know it. It's not even been twenty-four hours and I have managed to push her way. I want to tell her things, things that I feel and things that I think, but it's hard.

She waits patiently at the door for me to unlock it, her arms folded defensively.

"Maddison..."

"No, please Hendrix, you don't need to say anything. You've only just pieced your life back together and here I am invading that. I don't blame you at all for feeling frustrated."

I try to take her by the hand but she's quick to pull away. "But

I wasn't frustrated with you..."

"You don't have to explain." She's already grabbing some bits and putting them into her bag. I watch on, panicked, not knowing the right thing to say.

"Well, where will you go?"

"That motel outside of town, I'm sure the sign said that there were vacancies."

"No fucking way. Bates Motel looks better than that pit – there's probably a peep hole in the wall being used by a dodgy guy with no teeth."

That thought stops her in her tracks; she rolls her eyes and a little smirk forms in the corner of her mouth.

"Okay, well that's one way to put me off." She drops her bag onto the sofa and stares at me, trying to make sense of me. I know I'm not making it easy, and she deserves to know who I am.

"Let me run to the store, buy us some dinner, get some wine and we'll have a proper talk later."

She chews on her bottom lip in thought. "I don't want to outstay my welcome..."
"You couldn't, believe me. I do have some shit I'm still working on but none of it is to do with you, it's all me..."

***

Reluctantly, Maddison promised to stay. She must be feeling so uncomfortable, but I'm determined to fix that by the end of the night. I'll explain more to her about what I'm doing in therapy – I'll tell her that I didn't deal well with losing my parents, I'll even tell her how war made me angrier. I can't tell her about Martinez though, not now and probably not ever, but with everything else I'll try my best.

I throw some chicken and vegetables into the cart and decide I'll try my hand at that. I'm not much of a cook but it's one meal I used to make a lot, especially when I was weight training. I have no idea which wine she'll like so I choose one red, one white and a rose to be on the safe side.

For dessert I pick up a pumpkin pie, wondering if she's ever tried it; it's popular here in the States, especially the southern parts. It makes my mind wonder more about a future with her – maybe one day we'll be in England together and she'll show me where she grew up, she could make me crumpets, or scones or whatever English favourite she thinks I'll like. I know that I don't want a future without her in it and it scares me that I came to this conclusion so quickly, but deep down I knew from the first moment I met her that she was never going to be just a girl in a bar I met one night.

Just as I get to the checkout my phone vibrates in my pocket. When I pull it out and see the name, I'm automatically plunged into flight or fight mode. It's Evans, a fellow Marine Corp who I respected a lot; he retired not long before I was kicked out. I have no idea why he is contacting me now – he moved to Hawaii with his wife, so I doubt it's for a catch up over a beer. My instincts tell me it's bad news.

"Evans, hey, everything okay?"

The tone of his voice tells me instantly that it's not. My head swirls with the information Evans is trying to feed me: Jackson, a young new recruit I had taken under my wing, has killed himself. He was found hanging from the ceiling of his bedroom by his mother over the weekend. He was nineteen years old. Nineteen years old. God dammit.

I don't even recall saying goodbye, but I drop the phone back into my pocket and feel the dark mist cloud me. My hearing feels muffled, everything crowds in, the store suddenly looks distorted, and I know I'm about to have an anxiety attack. I ditch the cart but grab a bottle of Jack Daniel's on my way out, throwing down a twenty to a confused looking sales assistant. I must look like hell. As soon as I'm in the street I tear off the lid and gulp the brown liquor that stings my throat and heats my chest.

I picture Jackson on one of the last days I spent with him – he laughed as he told me a story about a prank involving clingwrap that he pulled on his cousin in the first week they joined us. He had this cheeky smile that got him out of any trouble. He was so full of life and so raring to go; he was keen, confident and a good guy. But a few months into deployment he began struggling with Afghanistan. He lost friends, he was homesick, he was scared. I took him under my wing, and it was my job to keep him sane, to help him turn it all around. But then Martinez happened and I lost my shit and ended up being kicked out. I couldn't support him anymore and now – now he's dead.

Nobody understands the things we see, the things we feel. Nobody understands how we still hear bullets being fired when we fall asleep at night, nobody understands that we constantly live with our fight or flight response at the surface. I understood though – I could have saved that kid, I could have stopped Jackson, I know I could have, but I wasn't there. I wasn't there because Martinez is a fucking monster and a rapist, and I snapped. I wanted to kill him.

I fall to my knees when I think of how different things could have been if I was different – if I had reported Martinez instead of beating him, I'd still be in Afghanistan, Jackson would still be alive, I'd have made sure of it.

I tilt my head back and gulp down as much whiskey as I can before my chest burns too much. I have to numb these thoughts; I have to numb the pain and the anxiety that is hanging over me like a black cloud. With every blink I see Jackson's smile, see him sitting on the edge of his rack, telling everybody in the camp funny stories. It's an image that makes my heart bang against my chest uncomfortably; guilt engulfs me as I feel the weight of responsibility. I stumble to the nearest bench, throwing back another shot.

CHAPTER THIRTY-NINE

MADDISON

Two hours. Two hours he has been gone and it's now dark outside. I thought we'd be finishing our dinner by now, maybe enjoying the wine on the porch and I'd be really getting to know Hendrix like I need to. But he is nowhere to be seen and I still don't have a phone so I can't even call him.

I've been pacing the lounge for forty-five minutes, trying to pluck up the courage to go looking for him but without my phone I'm scared. There's very minimal lighting around here and it's pitch black and wooded. I can't even Google to check if there's bears out there or wild wolves or something. I'm from England for god's sake – the scariest thing we have is a fox.

Oh god, what if he's had an accident? What if a bear got him? No, wait, he's in the truck, the chances of a bear attacking him are slim. I'm really driving myself mad here. Awkwardly, I begin searching through his drawers for a flashlight. Never in a million years would I have dreamt of going through his things, but desperate times call for desperate measures – if I wait any longer, I'll only convince myself of awful things.

Just as I'm rifling through the fourth drawer, I hear the sound of heavy boots plodding up the wooden steps to the porch.

I watch through the window as Hendrix staggers up the

stairs, before collapsing into the wooden chair. He takes a big swig from a bottle of whiskey before throwing it angrily onto the floor – it startles me enough that I jump back, watching as pieces of glass smash around him. I study him, trying to figure out what changed from the moment he left here to now. He doesn't have a single grocery bag with him, and I also can't see the truck, which makes me worry.

"Hendrix?" I call as I open the front door. "Did you have an accident in the truck? You've been so long..."

He doesn't even turn to look at me, he just keeps his head resting on his hand, staring into the distance. "No ma'am, just didn't want to drink and drive. Seemed like a nice night for a walk, don't you think?"

His words slur so much they trip over themselves.

"You're drunk? How? Why?"

"Because I'm an asshole. That's why."

I stand next to him, cradling my arms against my chest. I feel so sad to hear him like this, I've lost the Hendrix that I got to know, and I'm left with a version of him I don't recognise.

"Hendrix, I've been so worried. I thought you'd been in an accident or got eaten by a bear."

"A bear?" He turns to me with a vacant look in his eye. "Are there bears here!? Well fuck me, I wouldn't have walked if I knew that."

I'm not in the mood for humour.

"Please..." I feel a catch in my throat that I try to conceal, "tell me what's going on."

"You want to know what's going on?"

He pulls himself out of his chair and uses the wall to steady himself as he walks towards me.

"You want to know what's going on, Maddison?"

I nod, keeping eye contact.

"I'm destined to be fucked up, life has screwed me over and I almost, I almost thought I was catching a break when I met you." He pauses, studying my face. It's hard to see in the dark but his eyes look glazed over and I quickly realise they're tears that have gathered in his eyes. "You are the most beautiful person I have ever met in my entire life and I knew after we first met that if I ever got the chance to love you, I would do it with everything that I have, I'd give you everything you deserve, I'd make you feel so good that a lowlife like what's-his-name could never affect you ever again. But I can't, I let everyone down just like my dad let me down and that's why I'm not a fucking hero!"

"But we can help each other. You were there for me; I can be there for you too if you talk to me..."

"Okay, well I'm fucked up. Is that what you want to hear? The guy that saved you in the bar that night is a fucking mess inside and if I were you, I'd leave and never come back, because I'm a fuck up. That's it. That's all there is to know."

He glides past me and straight into the kitchen, banging around in the fridge and finding the last can of beer that was in there. I watch him helplessly as he self-destructs.

"Don't you think you've had enough?" I challenge him as he opens the can, but he acts like he doesn't hear me.

He pulls himself up onto the countertop, getting comfortable as he throws back the beer.

"Hendrix, come on, you've had enough." He ignores me again and I can feel myself growing more and more irritated with him.

I march over to him until I'm stood between his legs, and he has no choice but to look at me.

"What happened when you left here? Please talk to me."

His head shakes and his eyes drop to his feet, avoiding eye contact.

"Please..."

He places the beer down on the counter, brings both his hands up to cup my cheeks and looks at me properly for the first time since he came back. His eyes are red and puffy and his lips a little swollen.

"You're too good to know about the horrors I have inside my head." He says it so quietly it's practically a whisper. I step back as he jumps off the counter and walks away from me, looking like he is about to leave again.

"Please Hendrix, I need you to tell me, please don't just walk away..."

"I didn't want you to see this side of me..."

He stops, but he doesn't turn around. Both hands reach the back of his head, and he stands for a moment, silently, thinking.

Eventually he turns to face me; his arms drop to his sides and then he drops to his knees. "A kid I was taking care of in the Marines hung himself." And then he hangs his head in shame, a tear dropping from his cheek and onto his shirt. My heart aches watching his pain. I take two steps towards him just as he reaches up and wraps his arms around my waist. His head rests against my stomach and I wrap my hands around his shoulders, pulling him in tight.

"He was nineteen, he was a good kid..." His words come out desperate and sad, I can hear how at war he is with himself just by his voice. I don't even know all the ins and outs, but I know for sure this isn't his fault, he just feels like it is.

I stand, not moving, keeping my arms around him tightly, just allowing him to have a moment.

"Hendrix, this isn't your fault. I can only imagine how hard being a Marine is, I should imagine even the strongest minds have their moments..."

He pulls away from me like my words have left a bad taste. He walks straight back over to the kitchen and grabs the leftover beer.

"You don't understand. I should have been there. If I hadn't gotten kicked out, I *would* have been there, I would have helped him, I would have got him through it and his mom wouldn't be finding his hanging body! But I'm a fucking moron." He throws his half-empty beer can at the wall in front of him. "I got myself kicked out, I let my teammates down, I left that kid without help."

With that, he punches a cupboard door, which instantly swings back, hanging on by only one hinge. He yanks it off and throws it down onto the floor before punching the next door and pulling that off its hinges too. Suddenly, the noise in the room is extreme – his punches against the wood pound and bang and it startles me. I take a step back and another, until I'm backed against the wall, watching him helplessly.

"Hendrix!" I begin sobbing. "Please stop!"

He turns around, continuing his destruction. He flips the coffee table over and stamps on it until the wooden legs are just thin pieces of splint. He grabs the floor lamp and smashes it into a wall. I bring my hands up to cover my mouth. The panic in my breathing is loud, but I know he can't hear me, he has become sucked into his rage and it's like he isn't conscious to reality anymore.

"Hendrix!" Tucker bursts through the front door and leaps onto his cousin who is about to hit the television with the remainder of the floor lamp.

He pauses, looking in confusion at his out-of-breath cousin. Slowly he lowers the lamp from above his head and drops it to the floor.

"Take a breath, look at Maddison's face. I need you to look at her and snap out of it..."

He does just that and a breath deflates his chest, lowering his shoulders in the process as if something has just left his body. His eyes turn sad as he studies me again, seeing how I'm backed into the corner, crying.

"Maddy..."

CHAPTER FORTY

MADDISON

"I'm heading back to the lodge; I'll stay with Hendrix tonight; he's going to need support." Tucker says. Savannah nods approvingly at her husband and they share a kiss before he disappears down the road in his truck.

It's not even particularly cold but my body trembles as I stand beside Savannah; we have only just met properly – what an introduction!

"Come on, let's get some hot cocoa. Everything's better after a hot cocoa," she offers sweetly. I follow on behind as she leads the way into her beautiful white cottage. It has a huge wraparound porch and two swing seats; surrounding the porch are rows and rows of sleepers filled with vibrant coloured flowers. It could be a postcard; I can only imagine how beautiful it must look in the daylight.

Their ranch is also huge – I can see how it keeps Hendrix busy, there must be loads to do here. I sigh as my mind casually casts back to Hendrix, momentarily forgetting the disaster I just left. Everything happened so quickly once Tucker burst through the door. Apparently, he'd been to the store and one of the cashiers, who he obviously knew, it being such a small town and all, said she had seen Hendrix looking the worse for wear; she told him how he abandoned a cart of shopping and left only with booze.

From that, Tucker and Savannah both knew something bad must have happened and they went with their gut instincts – and I'm so glad they did because I didn't know what to do. I froze. I wasn't scared of him, nowhere close, but I was desperately sad and, worse, helpless. I didn't know whether to try and stop him smashing up the place or just leave him to get it out of his system; thankfully that decision was taken out of my hands when Tucker burst in. He practically rugby tackled Hendrix to the ground and, after a tussle, Hendrix paused long enough to realise what he was doing. He snapped back into reality and that was the most heart-breaking moment. His eyes followed the wreckage of smashed plates and bowls until they reached me.

I have to take a deep breath and stop myself from picturing his face before I start crying again; the image is too painful. He looked at me with such regret and shame, I just wanted to collapse on the floor beside him and hold him right back, the way he has been holding me when I've needed it. But Savannah ushered me out the door and before I knew it Tucker was driving us here, telling me I didn't need to see this side of Hendrix. Telling me that he'd only hate himself even more. But I don't think he should ever have to feel that way – we all break sometimes. He can't feel shame for losing it. Yes, it wasn't ideal, it was scary, and I was angry at first when I didn't understand where the hell he'd been or why he'd turned up drunk, but then he started opening up and I saw a glimpse of what he has been battling on his own.

I sit on one of the swing chairs, letting my feet float above the floor, feeling the light rocking relax me. In no time at all, Savannah places a mug of hot chocolate and a slice of apple pie in front of me. She has the southern hospitality down to a tee.

"I made it myself, it's one of my signature dishes, try some. I always think something sweet is ideal after a shock..."

"Thank you, it looks amazing, it really does, but I'm okay.

Hendrix doesn't scare me."

She smiles instantly, relieved to hear those words come from me.

"He doesn't scare me either – he scares the crap out of the rest of the town though! Excuse me for cursing."

I giggle at that fact – I can see why: he's big built and straight to the point. I can imagine he seems a handful to these small towners.

"Can I tell you something?" she asks, leaning forward like it's a secret.

"Of course..."

"Hendrix got into a fight within his first twenty-four hours of being here. Which wasn't a surprise, he has always been somebody who fights first and asks questions later. Probably why he was so good in the Marines – well, that and the fact he was never scared to die. He was so lost in this world that he figured he had nothing to lose, but that attitude only made him angry. That's the side of Hendrix we've always known. Then after Nashville, after he met you, he had this glimmer in his eye, like he had something in his life that was worth being here for..."

I can't put together a response straight away, I just sit quietly letting it sink in and thinking back to that night.

Savannah clutches my arm with a worried look. "I haven't made you upset, have I?"

I shake my head. "You definitely haven't. I was just thinking about that night." Savannah rests her chin on her hands, listening to me intently.

"When I was a kid, I was so obsessed with Dolly Parton! It started when my mum used to play her music but then I watched her on TV, and I was just in awe of her. She oozed confidence, with her big hair and bold look, she's just so fierce and, to me, she became an idol." I notice Savannah grinning as if I'm preaching to the choir – of course they all love Dolly here in Tennessee.

"I wanted to be like Dolly when I grew up. I wanted to be someone who knew what I wanted and wouldn't be scared to get it, someone who'd walk into every room fully confident with who I am, and I'd be, well, happy. But instead, I became nothing like Dolly. I've been floating around, trying so hard to make everyone else happy that I forgot about what I wanted."

"And what do you want?"

"I want to be a veterinary nurse, I want a fresh start for myself, I want to never ever have another relationship or friendship that makes me feel as bad as they did. I want to make myself proud and stop worrying about what people around me think. In fact, I need to start now." I stand up on a mission but turn to Savannah apologetically. "Please don't take this the wrong way because that's the best hot cocoa I have ever head, but I want to be with Hendrix, and I feel like he'd want that too. I can't sit here knowing the state he is in; I have to go."

I bend down quickly to give her a hug and before she has chance to say anything, I'm practically jogging across the grass and back towards the road. It's not far, if I keep power walking like this it'll be even quicker.

CHAPTER FORTY-ONE

HENDRIX

I haven't moved from the spot Maddison left me in. I don't blame her for going back to the ranch, I wouldn't want to be around me either.

Tucker's been sitting on the floor next to me, chewing my ear off, judging me and telling me off for drinking whiskey and ruining my life like I don't already know what the fuck I've done. I know what I have potentially lost and that thought sobered me up an hour ago when she walked out the door.

"Are you going to the funeral?"

I hadn't thought that far yet. "Maybe."

"You know how many people leave the Marines with mental health problems; you know you can't save them all. Jackson wasn't the first and it's sad, but he won't be the last."

I know that what he is saying is the facts. I know he is trying to make me see sense but it's hard when I feel like I could have at least saved him. I can't save everyone, that part is right, but if I had just finished this tour, I'd have spent enough time with him that I could have changed his thinking. He looked up to me a lot, I know I could have got him to talk to me.

"It hurts, Tuck," I say, my voice husky from the stress.

His hand comes up to squeeze my shoulder; his lips are pressed together, hiding his own emotion.

"I know, brother."

My head drops into my hands and I squeeze my eyes shut, trying to block the memories of this night out of my head just for a moment. Neither of us move. Tuck keeps his hand on my shoulder, I keep my head sunk in my palms and we just sit in silence. Thoughts of Maddison's face torment my mind, she's the last person I ever wanted to let down.

Tucker is the first to break the silence. "Erm, Hendrix… look."

It's Maddison. My jaw drops when I see her. I didn't expect to see her back here, especially not without me chasing her to apologise, but she's walking up the porch steps and to the front door. Fuck! I'm gawping in shock – she actually came back.

Something about her is different. She assertively lets herself in and her eyes lock with mine purposefully.

"Hey Tuck, could we have some time alone?" She asks the question but it's obvious it's just to be polite – it was rhetorical, she's telling him to leave.

Tucker stares between us uncertainly. He probably thought he'd be here all night picking up the pieces, hell, I did too. But she's proving us both wrong.

"Sure…" He's not sure though, but he gets to his feet anyway. "If anyone needs anything, just give me a shout."

I nod and Maddison smiles. As soon as Tucker shuts the door behind him, I realise I can hear my heart beating in my ears. I don't know if this is goodbye, but I know I wouldn't blame her if it was.

Her eyes scan the mess that I caused. I'm trying to read her, trying to understand what she is thinking but I can't get a sense of it.

"Maddison, I am so so sorry…"

"Hendrix, tell me one thing about yourself that you haven't

told anyone else before..."

I think for a moment but truthfully, I wouldn't know where to start. I could tell her that I'm in therapy, trying to learn how to solve my problems instead of looking for them in a whiskey bottle. But I think she's figured that part out about me.

"Okay..." I stand up straight, in the middle of all the disarray, and keep my eyes locked on hers. "I have liked trying to fix you because it made me forget how fucked up I am inside."

"Is that the only reason?"

The question is direct and confident.

"No, you know it's not, you blindsided me."

Her arms cross over the front of her body, and she pulls her grey t-shirt up and over her head, dropping it by her feet. "How?"

My eyes drop to her chest where a black lace bra elegantly supports her bust. I let my eyes follow the curves in her hips before bringing them back up to her chest and then her eyes.

"You gave me this feeling that maybe the world isn't so shit after all. You excite me..."

Her arm reaches behind her and without difficulty she unhooks her bra, revealing her beautiful breasts. Her eyes are still focused on mine.

"You don't scare me Hendrix..."

"I'd never want to..."

"I shouldn't have left you."

"No, Tucker and Savannah made the right choice. You don't deserve to see that side of me."

She takes a step closer to me. "I want to see every side of you. I want to be the one you run to instead of needing the whiskey, I want to be there for you like you've been there for me. All I could think when I was at Savannah's was..." A catch in her throat reveals her emotion, and she pauses, trying to compose herself.

I can't let her stand there and cry so I pace over to her, wrapping my arms around her waist and pulling her in.

"All I could think is that you've held me and made me feel safe. I want to be your safe place too. If you'll let me in?"

CHAPTER FORTY-TWO

MADDISON

I'm convinced he can feel my heart beating against his chest and when he tucks my hair behind my ears it thumps even louder, like steel drums. Hendrix tilts his head and his eyes study mine momentarily, waiting for permission to put his lips on mine. I lean into him, urging him to take control. And he does.

God, how can one person make you feel this good? I know there has been a spark between us but with each second that I feel his warm lips on mine a charge of electricity pulsates through my body.

With one swift lift, Hendrix has me off the floor and I wrap my legs around his waist and my arms around his neck as he carries me to his bedroom, keeping his lips on mine the entire time. He releases me down onto his bed with urgency – he wants me and I want him. As I lay back, his hands find my thighs and he grips them and pulls them apart, creating space for himself, making me gasp in excitement. Within seconds, he pulls off my blue jeans, leaving me in nothing but my thong. His eyes darken as he takes in my body; he stares at me hungrily, running his hands over my chest. My nipples harden under the warmth of his palm, a rush of heat stirs between my legs and I eagerly pull open his belt buckle and tug at his jeans until they're manoeuvring down his hips before dropping onto the floor. In a flash he pulls his black t-shirt up and over his head, revealing his chiselled body to me. My eyes scan all the tattoos that I haven't had the chance to see yet – so much artwork, so many meanings. Each one perfectly complements him.

He catches me admiring his body and smirks, before lowering down onto me and teasing me with his tongue, pressing gentle kisses into my hip bone, across my stomach and eventually back up to find my mouth. With one hand he slides his fingers into my knicker line.

"I want to make you feel so good." He whispers just as his fingers find my most sensitive spot causing me to gasp which he catches in his mouth. He kisses me faster, copying the rhythm of his fingers. My back arches into them and I feel so close to the edge, this built up sexual tension we've had has had me so ready for this.

I stop kissing him long enough to rush out the words, "I want you..." and my hands eagerly grip the waistband of his boxers and tug them down. Hendrix pulls down my panties with the same urgency and pauses again to admire me, like he wants to keep this image in his mind forever. I run my hands over his broad shoulders just as he pushes inside of me and releases a huge pleasurable sigh against my neck. I roll my hips into him, enjoying the pressure of him thrusting in and out of me. His mouth hungrily finds mine again and one hand grips onto my hip, holding me in place as our bodies grind together at the perfect speed.

Hendrix lets out the most delicious groan; it makes my whole body tingle. I could savour this moment forever. I feel so confident and sexy with Hendrix that it's giving me this whole new personality in the bedroom. In the past, I'd ask for the lights to be off and the covers to be over us, but with Hendrix, I want him to see every inch of me. The pressure of his rhythm and the way he hungrily kisses me brings me closer to the edge. Hendrix pauses kissing me just long enough to stare into my eyes and let me know that he has wanted this as much as I have.

"I'm getting close." I say flustered, my hand grips his back as the pleasure intensifies.

"Come for me…" He says against my lips before kissing me again. I love how in sync we are, how he reads how close I am. My body tenses around him and with two more deep thrusts, the pressure spills over and we both come beautifully undone.

He collapses beside me, getting his breath back, and stares at me with a huge grin. I don't think either of us thought that this was how the night would end. His thick arm wraps around me and pulls me in until I'm comfortably lying with my head on his chest, listening as his heartbeat goes back to a normal speed.

"You're really something, Maddison, do you know that?"

I smile to myself as my finger gently traces a scripture tattoo on his chest. His hand reaches down to my chin and tilts my head up until I'm lined up with his lips, then he leans down and gives me the most gentle and sensual kiss I have ever had; this time, he is slow and patient, savouring the moment.

He pulls away but keeps my chin in his hand. "Tell me something about you that nobody knows."

I think for a moment, and I have no idea if this is the most appropriate timing but all I can think about is how insecure I have been with Jamie and how this is so different.

"Okay…" I begin awkwardly. "This was the first time I have had sex with the lights on."

His eyebrow arches. "What do you mean?"

"I mean, before, I kept the lights off, or hid under blankets. My body had been under so much scrutiny with Jamie that I felt embarrassed any other way. I thought I was doing him a favour."

"Maddison…" His eyes look sad as he turns my body to face his. "Every inch of you is beautiful. I feel like the luckiest guy in the world with you in my bed and any douchebag who hasn't treated you like that before is a complete fucking moron."

I giggle. "But seriously," he continues, "it hurts me to think that you've had to feel that way."

I kiss him gratefully; I love how he makes me feel.

I want to ask him the question that I have been desperate to know: *why* he got kicked out of the Marines. I want to ask but I don't want to ruin this moment. This night had been horrendous, but it has somehow managed to end in the most beautiful way. I want to lie here peacefully, falling asleep together. I don't want to put pressure on him to tell me things he struggles with. One day, maybe, but not yet.

"Hendrix, I don't expect you to tell me all the things that haunt you right now, but I need you to promise me one thing…"

He sits up slightly, resting on his elbow and giving me his full attention. "Go on…"

"I need you to talk to me next time. Even if you don't want to tell me the actual problem, I need you to let me in and let me know you're struggling because smashing up this beautiful home wasn't the answer. It was hard to watch and I don't want to go through it again. I don't ever want your anger to ruin you. Promise me."

He sits fully up, taking me by the hand until I'm sitting up too. His eyes are serious but apologetic.

"Maddison, I have never had anything to lose before, until now, but I *promise* you, I am not going to let this thing take over me. I never want to put you through that again, I never want you to cry, not because of me. I'm so sorry. I won't break this promise."

I wrap my hands around his neck and pull him in close, tilting my head and relaxing it against his. "I know," I whisper.

CHAPTER FORTY-THREE

HENDRIX

I left Maddison sound asleep in my bed this morning, she looked so peaceful. She'll be pleased when she wakes up to see that almost all of the swelling around her eye has gone down and it's slowly turning back to a normal colour. She'll be relieved when she realises that.

Last night was amazing. Well, aside from the fact that I trashed my kitchen and allowed myself to succumb to my anxiety and neck another bottle of Jack, but I'm choosing to focus on only the positives that the night gave me. Maddison saw my battles and she came back. Maddison saw my rage and she wasn't scared. Maddison ended up in my bed, in my arms. I don't know what I have done to deserve her because quite frankly I don't think I do, but I'm grateful for her. I'm falling in love with her.

Today, I'm going to do something for her to let her know how grateful I am. Savannah sent me a text this morning and I realised that I could try and make this happen for her.

> *Morning. I hope you're both okay. I was thinking. Last night, Maddison mentioned how she wanted a career in veterinary. Do you remember Adelaide who came to Aunt Meryl's 50th? Well, she's the vet in town now, she has a clinic, I'll text you the address.*

Savannah x

So here I am, approaching the clinic with some oat milk latte that the barista assured me was a popular choice in hand to sweeten the deal.

As I walk inside, the clinical smell of disinfectant hits my nostrils. Posters of puppies and kittens cover every wall and as I approach the desk, I clock Adelaide kneeling down on the floor, rifling through some paperwork.

"Adelaide?" I catch her off guard and she jumps to her feet.

"Holy shit, Hendrix? Well I'll be damned. I heard you were in town, is it a flying visit?"

"Nope, I've bought a lodge here. I live here now." She smiles from ear to ear, taking in what seems to be great news.

She looks exactly the same as she did when I saw her last: blonde hair braided into two plaits, a tie-dye t-shirt with an animal print on it, today's choice is horses, and a pair of chunky combat boots, similar to mine.

"Savannah and Tucker must be so happy! This is such good news. I always hoped you'd move away from, you know... those memories."

She pauses guiltily as if she's made me feel awkward, but I smile reassuringly.

"I got you a latte."

Her face lights up. "For me?"

"Yep. I had no idea what to order, but the barista said this was a popular choice. How have you been anyway?"

She sips it gratefully. "Busy. Chad left; he met some girl in Vegas at a bachelor party. He reckons nothing happened but the hickey on his neck and the fact he came home with her underwear in his pocket says different."

I only met Chad once, at the 50th party, but I could tell he was a jerk. "Shit, I'm sorry…"

"It's okay, he was as worthless as gum on a boot heel anyways." I smirk at the strong southern charm in her tone. Only they could make an insult sound so poetic. "He left me with two beautiful boys and for that I thank God every day."

"Boys? I thought you had just Bryson?"

"I fell pregnant just before Chad left. I now have little Beau too. He's in the terrible twos and keeps me busier than a cat on a hot tin roof, but I love him anyway."

I try to make a mental note of these random southern expressions that I haven't heard before but I'm still getting used to *yonder.*

"I heard you're not in the Marines anymore?"

"No, I'm not," I sigh. "But I think it's been the best thing for me. I needed to get my head out of war, it was consuming me."

"It always does, then our country is left with a bunch of struggling veterans. Hey…" her eyes widen with an idea that's sprung to her mind, "you know they do meetings for guys like you every Thursday down at the library, right?"

"Guys like me?"

"Yep, ex-Navy, Marines, you name it, they're down there supporting each other. You should definitely go."

I didn't expect there to be much in the way of support in this tiny town but I'm glad there is. If I want to make Maddison happy, I have to help myself first. I don't know why I hadn't thought about something like this before, it makes sense to be around people who know what it was like over there. "Thanks Adelaide, I think I'll give it a go."

She smiles, pleased she's managed to help.

"Any chance you fancy helping me with one more thing?"

She smirks. "Go on…"

"There's this girl…" Her eyes light up, just like Savannah's did. "She's British, she's only going to be here for a couple of months, but she really wanted some experience in nursing animals. She was supposed to be in college doing a veterinary course, but things changed for her, and she didn't get the chance. Is there any way she can…"

"Of course! I could definitely use the help. Have her swing by here tomorrow lunchtime and I'll get her started. Be good to share some of the workload. I really need to spend more time with the boys."

It never fails to amaze me how quick people are to help around here. The southern hospitality strikes again.

I'm incredibly thankful and I let her know that.

CHAPTER FORTY-FOUR

MADDISON

Hendrix left me his phone with a note, thoughtful as always:

Good morning Maddison,

I could get used to waking up next to you. I have to pop out for a little while, but I've left you my phone in case you wanted to call your mom and let her know you're safe. Anything else you need to do on it, feel free. I'll see you real soon. H.

So much has happened in such a short space of time that I hadn't even thought about my mum, but she's the first person I call. I hold my breath for a beat as it rings but I relax when she answers cheerfully. She seems completely oblivious to everything, and I am so relieved that Jamie hasn't phoned her and freaked her out by informing her that I've separated from the girls. There's a first time for everything, I guess. I keep the call brief and upbeat, lying about losing my phone before changing the subject. I tell her a little bit about Nashville and how it was everything I hoped and then I pretend I have to go because we are about to visit another museum. She seems to buy it and sounds happy enough with my call. I decided not to tell her that I plan on staying for as long as the law allows me to without a visa; as far as she's concerned, I'll be home soon. I will tell her, but I just know it'll be a lot for her to understand – for whatever reason, she thought the sun shone out of Jamie's backside.

I'm in luck when I manage to get through to my bank, they inform me I just need to take my passport to a local bank here and they'll be able to release my savings for me. I'm so happy I could cry; I have felt like such a bum relying on Hendrix for everything. I start planning a meal I could cook for him, as a thank you.

Once I'm finished with the calls, I use the opportunity to take a nice long shower, hoping the warm water will relax me, and it works – for the first time in days, I feel a lot more at ease and optimistic. Even better, I catch my reflection in the steamed-up mirror; I wipe my hand across the condensation revealing a huge improvement around my eye. It's not puffy and it's not purple, all that remains is a little yellow from the almost healed bruise. It puts a spring in my step, so much so I'm actually looking forward to applying make-up today and feeling more myself.

I throw on a white tiered cotton dress and pair it with my cowboy boots. I then rummage through my suitcase and pull out my make-up bag, a little foundation and blush makes me recognise myself again. I add some mascara and a nude lipstick before tying my sun-kissed hair up into a messy bun – I love how the sun has made my highlights pop.

This morning feels so much lighter than yesterday already and every time I think about Hendrix coming back soon my heart skips a beat and I have to purposely stop myself from daydreaming about our sex last night. One thing is for sure, he was the best I've *ever* had.

***

It takes me about twenty-five minutes to reach the bank in town, but I enjoy every step of it. The skies are blue, the sun is shining and there's a light breeze keeping me cool. I manage to secure six hundred dollars of my money which will tide me over for now until I can get some work. I'm confident that I should be able to find something in this town.

By the time I make it back to the lodge, Hendrix is pulling

into the driveway in the truck. We smile brightly at each other.

"Where'd you go?" he asks as he jumps out of the truck.

"The bank, I managed to get some of my money."

"I could have given you a lift."

"On a day like this?! No way, the walk was perfect."

His arms reach around my waist, and he plants a soft kiss on my lips. He looks so much calmer and more content compared to last night.

"Let me take you out to dinner tonight?"

I roll my eyes playfully. "You're ruining my plan! I was going to surprise *you* with dinner, as a thank you."

"You think we're staying in when you look like *that?* It would be a waste. I found this impressive restaurant, so, say yes?"

I smirk against his lips as he kisses me again. "Yes, okay Mr Caine, I'll come to dinner with you."

He sweeps me off my feet and carries me to the porch like a husband carries his newlywed wife. I giggle the whole way, loving every second of this place we've reached together.

Carefully, he places me down onto the garden chair and takes a seat opposite me. He studies me, smiling and showing off his perfectly straight white teeth, before a more serious demeanour takes over.

"There's something I'd like to talk to you about, but there's no pressure. If it's a bit of a weird request, I'll understand if you don't want to."

I frown curiously and lean forward in my seat. "Okay?"

"I got a call on the way home to say that Jackson's funeral will be held the day after tomorrow. It's in Texas. I know it's a lot to ask but I wondered if you'd come with me?"

My heart melts and I leap out of my chair and wrap my arms around his neck. "Of course! Of course I'll come with you." I know how much of a big deal this'll be for Hendrix to even go and the fact he has asked me on top is a huge step.

"How far is Texas?" I ask into his neck, not letting go.

"About nine hours from here. I hope you know some good car

games…" I can feel the subtle rise of his ear against my cheek, letting me know he's smiling. I feel so close and connected to him right now. God, I'm falling hard for you Hendrix Caine.

CHAPTER FORTY-FIVE

HENDRIX

Maddison's eyes expand with amazement as she takes in the surroundings at the restaurant. We're seated in the patio area overlooking the green landscape. The views go on for miles and above us is a string of lightbulbs that drapes across the entire patio – it looks extremely romantic. If it hadn't been for Adelaide telling me about this place, I would never have known it was here, it's tucked away on the edge of town like a hidden gem.

Maddison added a red lipstick for the evening, and she looks unbelievably sexy. I can't peel my eyes from her. I watch as she smiles at the view, probably wishing she had her camera, but she doesn't mention it. She takes everything in, looking back at me every so often to see if I'm smiling too, and I am.

"Ooh, they have seafood linguine, that's one of my favourites." She continues scanning the menu approvingly. The sun is slowly setting behind the hills but gives off an incredible golden glow that lights up her entire face. I watch her for a moment, taking her in.

My parents would have loved her, my grandma especially would have been so happy to know that I finally met someone I care about. I wish they could have known I reached this point in my life.

I order a bottle of wine for the table, ready to surprise her with the good news that I managed to arrange today with Adelaide. As soon as the bottle arrives, I begin filling her glass first and then mine.

"Let's toast…" I say with my glass raised; Maddison arches her eyebrow for a beat but then lifts her glass to copy me.

I smirk, readying myself for her reaction. "To your new job…"

She takes a sip of her wine and almost chokes when the penny drops.

"Wait, what?"

"Well, there's a vet in town, her name is Adelaide and she's rushed off her feet. She could really use an assistant, someone eager to work with animals…"

Her hands immediately cover her mouth as she conceals a gasp.

"Really?!"

"Really," I nod. "She wants you to go down and see her tomorrow to discuss a start date."

Tears well up in her eyes. "I can't believe it, Hendrix," she sniffles between words. "I think that's the kindest thing anybody has ever done for me."

I can't help but laugh. "Don't thank me yet – we live in the country, I don't think it'll be all puppies and kittens, more like a lot of pigs and cows."

She taps her napkin gently at the moisture around her eyes. "I really don't care," she half laughs. "I love all animals and I'm so incredibly grateful just to have the chance to gain some experience. I don't even know what to say…"

"How about just kiss me?" She leans over without hesitation and pushes her lips against mine; her hand finds the back

HERO

of my head and she holds me in place as she takes her time kissing me passionately, not caring at all if we are being gawped at by anybody else.

She pulls away just enough to thank me before kissing me again. The feeling I get from making her this happy alters something inside of me. I don't just think about myself anymore, I think about her.

CHAPTER FORTY-SIX

MADDISON

Adelaide was a dream. She was incredibly sweet and easy to be around, just like Hendrix said she was. She offered me the job there and then and even promised to pay me in cash so that I can still earn a living. It's crazy – nobody would do that back home, but here, they care far more about each other than they do about the rules. And I love that.

I thought I'd only be an hour, but an hour turned into three and I'm only just heading back to the lodge. I helped Adelaide feed some bunnies she'd been nursing all week; they were taken in after their mother had been hit by a car. Then she picked up the boys from their nanny and I got to meet Bryson and Beau who were both incredibly cute and funny with their little southern accents.

If only Jamie could see me now – he was so convinced that I'd come here and fail, that I'd hate it and wouldn't be able to manage without him; he was so sure that I lacked the confidence, thanks to him, and wouldn't be able to do a single thing for myself. But I'm here and I'm doing it. Of course, I had a rocky start, but now I have a job, I have a place to stay and, most of all, I have Hendrix.

As I approach the driveway, I hear voices talking. I quickly work out that it's Hendrix and Tucker but what I can't work out is why Tucker is saying my name in a tone that makes me nervous.

"I'm *just* saying, you're falling for a girl who has to go back to England in a month. Is all this wise? You're going to end up worse than before…"

The sound of my feet on the gravel cuts off the conversation. I awkwardly approach them both sitting on the porch as if I hadn't heard anything at all. Hendrix stands up as soon as he sees me and I'm barely up the steps when he hugs me so tightly that my feet are momentarily lifted from the ground.

I glance at Tucker who looks at me uncertainly, like I'm the girl who's going to break his cousin's heart. I get it, he is scared for his cousin who has gone through so much, so I can't be offended that he wants to look out for him, but the realisation that I'll probably have to leave in a month suddenly makes me fear for the both of us.

***

In the truck, Hendrix reaches for my hand and pulls it onto his lap. I rest it there, comforting him. The closer we get to Texas, the more he seems to tense up. He has his military uniform in the backseat which he'll change into before we arrive. I have never seen Hendrix in his uniform, not even in a photograph; my heart flutters at how handsome I can imagine he'll look in it.

Last night was a little intense. I packed for both of us whilst Hendrix wrote a few things down on a notepad – at the last minute, a phone call had come through from Jackson's mother saying that she'd like someone to tell everyone a bit about what Jackson was like in the Marines. She thought the best person would be Hendrix. He agreed straight away but I could sense that the thought of public speaking about the Marines was way out of his comfort zone.

I want to bring up the conversation that I'd heard him and Tucker having yesterday, but I know today isn't the right time. I want to reassure him that even if I have to go back to England for a little while to sort things out, it doesn't mean I'm not coming back. There's a lot to think about going forward, but I know whatever I do, I don't want to do it without him.

The truck windows are wound halfway down; the only thing we hear is the breeze flowing through and the incredibly quiet background noise of the radio. It's been this way for at least an hour now. I keep trying to think of the right thing to say, but I'm not sure what that would be.

"I couldn't do this without you, Maddison," Hendrix says so quietly I barely catch it. When I realise what he said, I move my hand from his leg and instead rest it behind his head and the back of rest, stroking the base of his neck in the most affectionate way I can from my seat. For the first time in our journey, he puts on his black Ray-bans; I get the feeling it's to conceal emotion more than it is for the sun.

Hendrix swings the truck off the road and into the parking lot of a worn-out looking garage. "This gas station has bathrooms; I'll pull up here and we can get changed."

I step carefully inside the women's bathroom which is right next door to the gents. It's not the cleanest bathroom I've ever seen but it'll do. I take off my denim shorts and white t-shirt and place them to the side before taking my outfit from the bag and carefully pulling it over my head. It's a short-sleeved, black V-neck dress with a little leg slit in the side; it's very boho which has become my new favourite style recently. I put on some black ankle boots and, before I leave, quickly run my fingers through my natural curls and touch up my subtle make-up by adding a clear gloss.

I grab my clothes and pop them into my bag. As soon as I step outside, I see Hendrix standing by a tall tree. He has his back to me and is staring out towards the road, but in a beat, he turns around to face me, causing a rush of emotions. Somehow, he looks ten feet taller, stronger, noble and, as I imagined, so very handsome. I feel like I'm beaming with pride and admiration – he's an image of the strength this country offers, and I couldn't be more humbled to be in his presence.

"Wow..." I breathe.

"United States Marine at your service, ma'am," he jokes as he gives me the typical military salute. We catch each other's smile and pause for a second before Hendrix's eyes float from my eyes, down to my feet and back up again. "You look incredible."

"So do you. You've got this," I say as reassuringly as possible and together we get back into the truck and travel the last ten minutes to the church.

CHAPTER FORTY-SEVEN

HENDRIX

Maddison's delicate fingers intertwine with mine during the short walk to the church. I hear a few whispers already from people I toured with. I wonder if she does too, but if she does, she's not letting it show.

"I heard he put him in a wheelchair."

"Apparently the fight was over a Superbowl game, he's crazy."

"I thought he was in jail."

"I hear he's schizophrenic and poor Martinez caught the brunt."

The whispers make me tense up and I grind my teeth to stop me from turning on these guys and telling them what the fuck really happened, but I wouldn't, today is for Jackson, nobody else. I'm out of the Marines now anyway and my life is the polar opposite to who they thought I was back then. I don't care what they think of me now, I'll let them think what they want. We get through the crowd and step inside the church. Jackson's family sit in the first couple of rows; his mom sobs as she stares at the American flag draped over her son's casket. Maddison gives my hand a little squeeze; she's become the rock I hadn't realised I needed.

As I would expect for a Marine funeral, the church is pretty packed. Every American wants to pay their respects to their local hero, it's their way of saying thank you. Photos of Jackson as a young boy are projected onto a screen, soft music plays and lots of sobs are heard. He was a blond-haired, blue-eyed boy who looked like his little grin could get him out of anything – and I think it did. Jackson helped himself to the last of my chocolate stash plenty of times, but I could never stay mad. He definitely used his charm to avoid a beating plenty of times. It's hard to watch his mom so distraught, it takes me back to my parents' funeral – I heard the same sounds, the sounds of people trying to hold it together, the sounds of hearts breaking and the sounds of the last goodbyes. It's hard.

The speeches are underway and it's his mom who struggles the most, managing to read only half of her letter before breaking down; her husband takes over. Knowing it is soon my turn makes my chest tight and my throat dry. I don't even know if what I wrote down is good enough, I just hope it is. I keep glancing at the huge portrait of Jackson next to the casket – he's in his uniform, smiling brightly, so full of life. He had so much to look forward to.

"Next," Jackson's father begins, "we have some words from Hendrix, a man my son looked up to a hell of a lot." His arm extends as he gestures for me to join him at the front.

I slip my hand out of Maddison's and rise to my feet. I suddenly realise how far back we are sitting because the walk to the front is long and all eyes are on me, half for the right reasons and half because they think I'm an unstable schizophrenic who tried to murder a fellow Marine.

As I approach the stand I clear my throat, mostly because it feels thick with emotion and I need to stay composed. Jackson's mom is watching me, and I can't let her down.

"For those who don't know me," I start, pulling out the notes from my pocket, "my name is Hendrix Caine. I have enlisted and re-enlisted since we were brutally attacked on 9/11 and I have had the honour of meeting some incredible men and women along the way, but Jackson for sure was the youngest." I pause, staring at the paper, before taking a breath and continuing.

"For years now, our country has watched as men like Jackson step up and defend our nation. A lot of us in this room have killed for our country, faced terrifying fear for our country and risked death in every war we fought. Not only did Jackson do all that but he had this incredible gift where he could still come back at the end of the day and make us all laugh. Now I realise that he was a kid who was scared and hurting inside too, but he put that aside to help everybody else to feel some relief. Knowing he could make somebody else smile on their darkest days gave him comfort. If you've known Jackson, then you've known Greatness."

I catch a glimpse of his mom smiling and I feel relieved that my speech is doing that for her.

"If I could say anything to Jackson it would be this: you always said it was a privilege to be a Marine, but it was my privilege to be your brother. The world was a better place because you were in it, so believe me when I say this, because I don't use this word lightly, but you were and always will be a Hero." The room applauds. I didn't expect it, but I fully embrace it.

"May your soul rest," is the last thing I say into the microphone before walking away.

Maddison has tears in her eyes as she claps me proudly. When I finally reach her, I kiss her on the forehead. I'm so relieved I got through it, but mostly I'm happy I gave Jackson the speech he deserves.

"You couldn't have said it any better," Maddison tells me as soon as we are back outside again.

I rest my forehead against hers as she smiles up at me. "I couldn't have done it without you."

Her arms reach around me, knowing how much I needed this moment. I bask in it for as long as I can before we watch

Jackson for the final time as he is lowered into the ground.

Rest in Peace, Axel Jackson, I'll miss you.

CHAPTER FORTY-EIGHT

MADDISON

It's been a couple of days since the funeral and, as my holiday time had virtually run out, I had no choice but to phone my mum yesterday and tell her the truth – that I was not at the airport about to board my return flight home, but instead I had met someone, who I like a lot, and that I'm currently staying with him in his home in rural Nashville and I've illegally obtained a job. Okay, I didn't quite say the last part – one thing at a time. After a lot of questions about Hendrix and whether or not I think he's going to murder me in my sleep, she ended up saying that she was happy if I was happy. Which is actually the first time she's said anything like that, so I'm taking it as a win.

Despite it being very early days, my job at the moment is unreal. It's so good that it makes me sad to think I actually gave up that dream for so long for Jamie, but immensely grateful for Hendrix. I love so much that he remembers everything that I tell him, and he genuinely roots for me to make all my goals and dreams come true. He cares, like *really* cares.

Yesterday I was left to nurse the bunnies by myself and today Adelaide is letting me check over one of the pregnant pigs at the ranch. Tucker called in this morning to say she's not eating, and I am being entrusted with the huge task of seeing whether I can form a diagnosis. I read so many books on animal anatomy when I was getting myself ready for university and I hope I can remember some of what I read.

I walk to the ranch with a notepad and pen so that I can make any relevant notes I need to for Adelaide – I practically skip there, the excitement to finally be working with animals is exhilarating. I'm barely inside the barn when a pair of strong arms grab me from behind and I feel a kiss on my neck, sending goosebumps through my body.

Tucker rolls his eyes but smirks at the sight. "Hey, put her down! We got work to do."
Hendrix does as he is told but not without flipping his cousin off first. They make me giggle, they're like unruly siblings who can't stop winding each other up for five minutes.

"So where is she? Where's the pregnant pig?"

"Now that's not a nice way to talk about my wife!" Tucker teases as my face goes bright red. I playfully shove him out of the way, making Hendrix laugh.

"We had to separate her from the others in case she's got something contagious. I'll take you to her," he continues, leading the way.

I glance back at Hendrix who is still smiling at our banter but gets back to work.

Along the way Tucker fills me in about her behaviour, explaining that she isn't moving very much, she's not eating, and she seems stressed. I make sure to keep a mental note of it all. She's in a little homemade pen with a tin roof and wooden fence; it looks very cosy but he's right to be concerned, she's not looking happy at all, the poor thing is lying in her own mess and looks incredibly lethargic.

I take her temperature and listen to her heartbeat, check her eyes and look for signs of porcine parvovirus. Thankfully, it doesn't seem to be that – good thing too otherwise she'll likely have a stillbirth.

"Well, there's good news and bad news," I announce. "It's not parvo or anything like that but it does look as though it could be the gastro-virus. It won't kill her but if her litter are born and they try feeding from her, it'll likely kill them."

"They'll need to be hand-reared?"

"Yes and taken from her immediately. If they're with her too long they'll catch it and be too weak to fight it."

"Shit, I best set up a camera so I can keep monitoring her through the night," Tucker says but he's talking to himself and making mental notes more than he is talking to me. "I'll make up a bed indoors, ready for their arrival."

"I'll get Adelaide to come up and confirm later today. I also don't mind staying and keeping an eye on her in case she goes into labour."

"Really? God Maddy, that'll really do me a favour, especially as I need to go out and get supplies now."

I nod. "I'm more than happy to help."

***

Hendrix watches me in amazement as I pace across his living room, telling him all about the pig. "And that's when I worked it out, that it's gastro, and Adelaide confirmed it before I left so at least now we know we need to get prepared for the litter."

He stretches his arms and rests them behind his head, not taking his eyes off me.

"Oh! And then Savannah was so relieved that I have potentially saved the piglets that she's making me a Victoria sponge cake!"

"A Victoria sponge cake?"

"Yeah, it's a traditional cake in England. I think she googled it and assumed I'd love it."

Hendrix can barely conceal his laughter. "And do you?"

"Sure," I shrug. "The point is, I done good right!?"

"So good babe, now come here." He reaches out his hand and pulls me towards him on the sofa. I get comfortable, slipping my leg over his and resting my head on his chest; his fingers stroke the hairs away from my face and we just relax into each other.

"Maddison…"

"Yes?"

"I love you…"

My chest swirls, my heart skips a beat and I lie there momentarily, smiling from ear to ear. He loves me. This guy told me he has never loved in all his adult life and here he is, confessing his feelings for me. I don't need to think about my feelings, I have no doubt that these feelings growing inside me only amount to one thing.

"I love you too…"

CHAPTER FORTY-NINE

HENDRIX

"The love-bomb huh? Already?" Tucker scratches at his chin, taking it all in.

"When you know you know right? That's what you always told me. How did you know Savannah was the one?"

He smiles to himself, reliving a memory. "Life was just better around her."

"That's how I feel! She's like a drug, every time I'm with her I feel so differently about the world. For the first time in my life, I don't despise it. All I have ever known is loss, terror and war. But with Maddison, I want to learn about the other side of life – love, marriage, children, the whole nine miles."

Tucker smiles. "Grandma would be so happy if she could hear this."

"Yeah, she pretty much suspected I'd be a lost cause."

"Oh, she didn't just suspect – she asked me and Savannah to build an extension where you could live out your years as a sad old bachelor!" He bursts into laughter.

I match his laughter. "Fuck! I was *that* bad?!"

"The worst! I was starting to think you'd need to be visited by three ghosts to snap you out of it."

I throw my water bottle at him playfully; it's the only thing I can grab in the barn. He manages to catch it and gives me a smug look.

"I think at one point we all assumed you'd wind up in prison, although I suppose you came very close to that." His tone turns serious. "Does Maddison know about that yet?"

I shake my head.

"Well, I know it's bad from the snippets you've allowed us to have. Perhaps Maddison should be the one you finally open up to about it."

"Not if I can help it Tuck, that image isn't one she deserves to have in her head. No one does, but least of all her. I'm not going to plague her with that shit."

He nods. I know he doesn't fully understand seeing as I've never told him the ins and outs, but he's not stupid, I think he can guess how bad it was.

"How long has she got left here?"

I squeeze my eyes shut for a beat, not really wanting to think about it. Even though it's *all* I keep thinking about. "Three weeks and three days."

Tucker ponders for a second. "Savannah was doing some research and even though she has to leave after ninety days, she can literally come straight back for another ninety days."

I absorb the information. "So, there's no waiting time until she can come back again?"

"Nope, in fact Savannah said she technically doesn't even have to go back home, you guys could take a drive over the border into Canada and come back. It still counts."

"Tuck, I could kiss you!"

He curls his top lip in disgust. "Please don't."

"I can't wait to tell her that she doesn't have to give up this job that she loves so much. I'll just book us a weekend trip to Toronto or somewhere, and then we can have another ninety days unbothered."

"Yep, and you can thank me by staying on another hour tonight. I've got to take Savannah to the hospital for a scan."

I'm not thrilled to be late home to Maddison, but he deserves my help – after all, he puts up with my shit. "Of course, I'd do anything... for Savannah." He pretends to be offended but quickly laughs it off.

I phone the clinic and my heart skips a beat as soon as Maddison answers. I explain that I'm watching the ranch for a while tonight so that Tucker and Savannah can attend their hospital appointment.

"No problem at all," she answers. "Works out well actually because Adelaide said the boys are with their grandparents tonight, so she's asked me to have a few drinks with her at the bar. You don't mind, do you?"

I laugh. "Of course I don't, but you'd better not leave me for a cowboy."

"Never," she giggles but answers without hesitation.

I spend the afternoon getting the horses outdoors and into their field and cleaning out their stables. I can't wait to see Maddison tonight, I can't wait to tell her all the information Tucker gave me. I'm counting down the hours until I can see her face. We agree to meet at the bar when I'm finished up here.

***

Savannah waves me goodbye as they pull away in the truck. Her eyes sparkle with anticipation, her hospital folder clutched tight to her chest. She's wanted this for so long. I watch them drive away, feeling emotional. I couldn't be happier for them. That's my family. I always felt I was lost because I didn't have much – I had no parents, my grandmother died when I was deployed, and I had no siblings. I realise now I had the best family right under my nose. I have Tucker who has always been more of a brother than a cousin anyway and I have Savannah who has been a sister to me – and now I have Maddison. It's incredible how life can change when you just hold on. The number of times I abused whiskey and hoped it would take me in my sleep, but that feeling is so far from what I want now. I'm here, I'm living and, dare I say it, I'm happy.

CHAPTER FIFTY

MADDISON

I'm having the best time with Adelaide, she's infectiously positive. Even the way she talks about her ex-husband cheating and leaving her to raise the boys, she says it as if it's all part of God's plan. I'm not religious in the slightest but I admire so much how her faith has given her this outlook on life – she trusts that it's all part of a process and that it's a path to a better life. She asks me about my past love life, and I tell her bits and pieces about my relationship with Jamie. I love how I haven't got to go into too many of the nitty gritty details because she just gets it, she worked him out real quick and nods along as if everything I'm saying makes so much sense.

"He sounds like a typical narcissist. He'll probably never love anyone as much as he loves himself. But you know what is cool about being with someone like him?"

I sip at my wine, listening.

"It makes you so grateful when somebody loves you right – you *know* how good you've got it, and you don't take it for granted."

I immediately think of Hendrix of course. I think back to how I catch him staring at me, I could be getting changed or just washing up after our dinner and I feel his eyes on me, they're always hungry for me and I know he is admiring me. If Jamie ever stared at me for too long, it would be to tell me I'm not slim enough.

"I'm certainly grateful for Hendrix," I finally say. "I couldn't be without him now."

She nods enthusiastically. "And he must feel the same because he has calmed down so much since being with you! I mean, I obviously haven't seen it first hand, but Savannah would tell me about his temper and how it would land him in trouble."

"I don't know much about it either, but he is letting me in, slowly."

I decide not to mention that he smashed his kitchen a couple of weeks ago, partly because it isn't anyone else's business but also because I don't see that as Hendrix. The Hendrix I know is caring, compassionate, fiercely protective and loving. He is working hard to be the best version of himself every day and I am too. We are both a work in progress and are helping each other to achieve that. He is making me feel confident and attractive so that the timid and self-conscious version of myself is becoming a distant memory. And I'm helping him to see that he is worthy, he is loved and that he deserves to experience the good that life has to offer.

She smiles brightly. I'm growing really fond of Adelaide. She's the type of person you could tell anything to and there'd be no judgement.

"Anyway, I'll get the drinks this time, same again?"

***

We are enjoying our third glass of wine and I am lost in the dramatic stories Adelaide has to tell about the animals she's worked with, most of which seem to have involved hamsters, which makes me chuckle. I think back to my first hamster. I called her Sarah after my favourite witch in *Hocus Pocus*. She somehow escaped once and I couldn't find her for three days. I searched the house from top to bottom, making Mum and Dad help me too, but she was nowhere. Then casually in comes our cat one evening with Sarah hanging out of her mouth. It was traumatising to say the least, but then again nearly every story involving hamsters is.

"Oh snap!" Adelaide suddenly covers her mouth in shock. "I don't think I locked the bunnies' cage door."

Our eyes widen as we imagine a clinic full of baby bubbies wreaking havoc.

"Don't worry, I'll go," I offer.

"Are you sure?"

"Of course! You enjoy your well-earned child-free evening. I'll walk down there and check and then come back."

"Oh, you're a peach!" She gives me a grateful smile as she hands me the keys and I head off on my way.

I'm surprised at how windy it is when I step outside, a storm must be brewing because I haven't known it to be quite like this before. All the fresh air makes me feel light on my feet – I think those three glasses of wine are taking effect.

It's quiet on the street as always, but I spot a man near the bus stop I was at when I first arrived. I don't recognise him, he's tall and quite muscular, a similar build to Hendrix really.

He catches me staring and uses it as an opportunity to wave in my direction as if he wants me to stop. I do to be polite and he starts walking over to me.

"Hi!" he says with a friendly smile. His accent tells me he isn't from the south.

"Hello?"

"Sorry, I was hoping someone could help me. I'm looking for an old buddy."

"Oh!" I feel relaxed now, knowing that he is just lost like I was when I first got here and not some dangerous stranger lurking at bus stops. "I'm a bit new here myself, but I can definitely try to help."

He looks relieved. He keeps his smile and looks around him briefly to make sure nobody is in earshot before he tells me the name.

"My buddy's name is Caine, Hendrix Caine, do you know him?"

My face lights up. Hendrix always seems like such a lone-wolf, he has never mentioned a friend before. Even at Jackson's funeral he mostly kept himself to himself, apart from some small talk with a few.

"I'm staying with Hendrix," I announce proudly and extend my arm to shake his hand. "It's nice to meet you...?"

"Luis, Luis Martinez," he answers as he shakes my hand.

"Nice to meet you Luis. I've just got to pop to the vet clinic down the road and then we'll go back to the bar if you like? Hendrix is meeting me there soon."

He smiles gratefully. "I'd like that, thank you."

Together we start walking to Adelaide's clinic. "So, you must be his girlfriend then?" The question catches me off guard.

"Yes, well, it's early days, but yes, he's my boyfriend."

"That's cool, I didn't really think he had it in him."

"Oh?"

"Yeah, he just never seemed the settling down kind of guy. They had a name for him in the Marines."

I register the last part the most. "You were in the Marines together?"

"Yep. He was known as the seducer, because somehow, he just knew the right thing to say to a woman to make her drop her knickers. They'd think he was something special and then he'd chuck them as quickly as he seduced them. Sad really, I was brought up to have more respect for women than that, but hey, that was a few years ago now."

I nod, not really knowing what to say. Everyone has a past, and I know Hendrix had a few one-night stands, he told me about them. But it's different now, he said that too.

"Don't Marines have a reputation for being party boys during their leave?" I ask breezily, attempting to make light of the topic. Picturing Hendrix leading on multiple women just for sex doesn't exactly fill me with joy.

He laughs. "You're right there. We all have a story or two I suppose."

"Well," I shove the key into the lock, "we're here. I've just got to make sure these bunnies are locked safely away and then we'll find him. You can come in and wait."

I flick the light on and make my way out back. Luis hovers in the waiting area, staring at the posters. I'm relieved when I get to the back and see all the bunnies are accounted for; they're all cuddled into each other asleep, which makes my heart melt as I watch them. I slide the metal lock across to secure them inside and when I'm happy they're fine I head back to find Luis.

He's seated on the receptionist chair, legs relaxed, hands behind his head, looking a bit too comfortable for my liking.

"Shall we go?" I prompt, heading back to the front door.

"Wait," he calls. "Let's talk more about Hendrix first."

CHAPTER FIFTY-ONE

HENDRIX

The wind has picked up so much that I'm having to take the horses back inside. Tuck called to say they've issued a tornado warning in three counties, so they've decided to stay at the hospital until it's been lifted. Smart move, I wouldn't fancy being on a freeway when a twister comes along either.

I hear the rumbling of thunder in the distance – a big storm is definitely on the way and it makes me want to get back to Maddison urgently. She's probably never witnessed a tornado before, I'm pretty sure England doesn't get them, and she may not realise how dangerous they are. We don't really get them on the east coast, so it isn't something I have a tonne of experience in either, but I'm American, I know well enough of the damage they can do.

With the animals secure and shut away, the only one left I have to worry about is the pig. She could go into labour at any moment, and someone needs to keep an eye on her, especially with all the noise from the storm; if she gets stressed it'll be even worse for her.

Maybe I should get Maddison and come back here to keep an eye on her. We should be safe – if it looks as though a tornado is coming our way, we'll just head into the cellar.

By the time I get to my truck, the rain and hailstones are battering down onto my windshield. It's deafening and makes it extremely hard to drive; the windshield wipers can't keep up with the speed of the rain, meaning my screen is one big blur. It forces me to drive painfully slowly.

Town is deserted by the time I reach it; most people have probably heard on the news that we're on tornado watch and gone straight home. I park my truck right beside the bar and run inside. It only takes a few seconds but I'm dripping wet by the time I step inside.

"Wow!" Adelaide gasps with a laugh when she sees me. "Little wet out there huh?"

"Just a touch," I answer, wiping droplets from my brow. I scan the bar; it's pretty quiet for obvious reasons but I can't spot Maddison anywhere.

"Where is she?"

"Oh, she had to pop to the clinic to check the bunnies were locked away, my scatterbrain may have overlooked it. She should be back in a second, sit down, I'll get you a drink."

"I can't, I've got to get straight back to the ranch and look after the pregnant pig."

"Sow."

"Huh?"

"A pregnant pig is called a sow. It just sounds nicer than pregnant pig."

I smirk, she's not wrong.

"Are you sure you should go back to the ranch now? We're on tornado watch. Earl says he's going to lock up in a minute and if it gets really bad, we can sit and wait it out downstairs."

Earl must be the guy who owns the bar. I've been here a few times, but this is the first time I've heard his name.

"It should be okay if we leave now. Tucker will kill me if I don't keep an eye on this pig, sorry, sow." Adelaide giggles.

Pete, who I didn't even notice was sat right in front of me, spins around in his bar chair. "Well Marine boy, you might have a fight on your hands."

I roll my eyes at him; he's drunk and seems to want to drag me into a sparring match as usual.

"And why's that?" I humour him.

"She was walking down the road with another man earlier. Seemed more her type too." He winks, trying desperately to get a rise out of me. I look at Adelaide who just shrugs and looks as confused as I do.

"She left here alone," she informs me. "What are you talking about Pete?"

"I went out for a smoke and some guy went over and started chatting to her, looking for you by all accounts. Is he here to kick your ass? Lord, I hope so."

"Oh, behave yourself, Pete!" Adelaide chimes in.

I can't think of anyone who would be here looking for me. Nobody knows where I am, apart from my therapist and a few buddies I briefly chatted to at the funeral, but none of them would come here.

"What guy? What did he look like?"

"Ooh, nervous are you, Marine boy?" His eyes are gleaming, smug that he is winning the game I didn't want.

"Pete…" Adelaide sighs restlessly.

"Okay, okay," he gives in. "Martino I think he said, something exotic like that anyhow."

The name is like a punch to the throat. I feel winded. "Martinez?"

"Yeah, that's the one."

I dart for the door, my heart racing at an uncomfortable

speed. All sorts of things run through my mind and I can't think straight. Why is he here? How did he find Maddison? Is she okay? What if he is hurting her?

The wind is strong and the rain heavy, but I sprint down the street as fast as my legs will carry me. Images of Maddison crying like that girl did back in Afghanistan flash into my mind. I'll kill him. If he has touched a hair on her head, I won't be able to stop myself this time, I know it. I'll kill him.

CHAPTER FIFTY-TWO

MADDISON

His demeanour has changed and I'm growing uncomfortable. He keeps referring to Hendrix as his pal, but his tone is unkind, like he has some problem or a score to settle.

Luis still sits swinging from side to side in the chair. He lifts his feet from the floor and plonks them down onto the desk, completely disregarding all the paperwork that's on there.

"Erm, would you mind removing your feet?" I try to say it confidently but I'm not sure it delivers that way.

He smirks, not moving an inch, and stares at me like I'm pathetic. I'm not sure who I have let in or who I am talking to, but there's no way Hendrix would be *buddies* with someone like this.

"So, how long has my boy Hendrix been fucking you for?"

His words send a chill down my spine. "We met in Nashville last month, if that's what you're asking." He throws his head back like I've said something hilarious.

"That's cool, so you've followed him down here to this hillbilly town in the middle of butt fuck nowhere?"

"Look, my friend is waiting for me. I have to lock up..."

"Has Hendrix told you yet why he got kicked out of the

Marines? I'm guessing not otherwise you'd know who I am. Do you want to know why?"

I shake my head. "I'd rather he told me, when he is ready."

He moves his feet back to the floor and stands up, keeping his eyes on me, still smiling smugly. "I'd rather tell you, if you don't mind."

Something about him is off – his eyes are cold and I'm growing scared. I turn to open the front door but just as I go to do it, his arm darts forward and slams it shut again. He grabs me hard by the arm and pulls me back, causing me to stumble and fall. He doesn't bat an eyelid that I'm now on the floor.

"He was jealous of me, I realise that now, that's why he wanted to ruin me. The guys looked up to me, I was one of the best in our field, my future was sure looking bright, until he snatched it away. He accused me of something, something so sinister that it got everybody talking and soon enough I was granted medical leave. Do you know what that means?"

He towers over me and I can feel the tension from him, like he could explode at any moment. I feel so trembly that I can't bring myself to answer; I shake my head instead.

"It basically means I was forced out of the Marines because they think I lost my fucking shit. They were worried I was crazy. So that's that. Thanks for your service, Luis Martinez, but the United States no longer needs you."

I pick myself up off the floor, trying desperately to hide my fear. "I don't know what happened, I'm not the one you should be speaking with."

He pauses, staring at me with an unkind smirk that sends a shiver down my spine. "Is that a British accent?"

"Yes…" I sigh.

"That's sexy as hell." He reaches his arm around and squeezes my bum-cheek. The grip is unforgiving, and it hurts. I push his hand away and attempt to get past him, but he grabs me by the throat and pushes me back onto the desk.

"I wasn't sure how I was going to make Hendrix pay for ruining my career – and then you came along. It's like a sign isn't it? What better way to settle a score than with somebody he cares about?"

I gulp, tears rush to my eyes and my bottom lip quivers. The air in the room feels like it has been sucked out. I feel smothered by him as he towers over me. He keeps his perverted gaze on me as he unzips his trousers.

"Don't," I sob. "Please, I just want to go."

He doesn't hear my words, his eyes are vacant and soulless as he tugs hard at my t-shirt, causing it to rip and reveal my chest. He looks impressed at himself as he drops half my t-shirt onto the floor. His eyes gawp at my breasts and a smile corners his mouth as his hand reaches up and cups my breast aggressively. Inside I'm so scared, I'm dizzy; my mouth is dry, and I feel like I could pass out.

"Please, stop," I cry one last time, hoping to pull at his heart enough that he realises what he has gotten himself into, but it's clear he doesn't have one.

He leans forward and places his lips against my neck. I freeze in fear, tears falling down my cheek as his mouth widens, sucking in my skin before he bites down hard, causing me to scream out in pain.

He laughs, taking pleasure in my pain.

His arm slips around my waist and he flips me over until I'm face down on the desk. He lifts my white skirt until it's above my waist and kicks my legs wide apart.

"This'll hurt," he sneers, "feel free to bite down on something."

CHAPTER FIFTY-THREE

HENDRIX

My heart is in my throat when I get to the door – it's wide open and the waiting room is in disarray: there's blood on the floor, a smashed lamp and parts of Maddison's t-shirt.

"Maddison!" I shout out desperately at the top of my lungs. There's no answer but I see a familiar boot poking out from behind the desk. It's Martinez.

He's propping himself up against the wall and has a rag pressed against the side of his head where blood pours from, but he is still quick to get to his feet.

"She's fiery your new girl isn't she?" He's smug as he knows he has found my weak spot by using Maddison against me.

My teeth are gritted. I'm seething and it's taking everything I have not to rip his head off. "What happened?"

"Don't worry, she smashed me in the head with a lamp before we got to the good stuff."
A wave of relief comes over me – she fought back.

"Those tits though…" He winks and I leap from where I'm standing and tackle him to the ground.

"Did you fucking touch her?"

He sneers looking disgustingly pleased with himself. "I ran my hands all over her tits, I bent her over and felt her pert little ass against my cock." He bursts into laughter just as my fists ball up and I rain down on him, one punch after the other, my adrenaline is powerful and scary, like it was back on that horrible day, my brain isn't thinking, my body is jumping into action, I slam my fist against his jaw, his tooth cuts into his lip and blood spatters his face.

"Do it!" he laughs, "kill me and go to prison for the rest of your life. Do it Hendrix!"

He urges me on, lying there and taking my beating. A flash of Maddison comes into my head – she's standing in my kitchen, asking me to promise her that I'll never let my anger ruin me. If I don't stop now, I'll let us both down. Watching Martinez get the beating he deserves will only feel good for a minute, but a life with her is not worth compromising for that minute. I push myself off him and lean back into the wall, catching my breath.

"Come on Hendrix, you've got more than that in you…" His attempt at goading me isn't going to work, not when I have Maddison's face pictured in my mind.

"So I can go to prison this time, huh? That's what you want isn't it."

He nods and smiles revealing the puddle of blood between his lips.

I bring my knees up, resting my arms on them and staring at the monster in front of me.

"You lost it man, somewhere over in Afghanistan, you lost your mind," I say. I don't even recognise him to be the man I first met. "It got you good, the fear, the terror, it got into your head."

"Fuck life before it fucks you," he sneers, not moving from the floor, "isn't that the motto?"

I shake my head at his words.

"You ruined me Hendrix, you know that right? You should do."

"You ruined yourself."

The blood must have run to the back of his throat because his words are gargled. "It was just a fuck."

"No, it wasn't. It was a Marine going against what he'd been trained to do and taking advantage of a terrified woman. You don't deserve to represent our country and if I had killed you, it would have been one less rapist in the world and I would have slept soundly."

For the first time, there are no smug comments; he doesn't laugh, or antagonise, he just stays silent.

"I became the bad guy like the ones I thought I was fighting against, didn't I?" he chokes out. Reluctantly, I grab him, propping him up so he doesn't drown in his own blood.

He smiles. "Marine through and through aren't you, always ready to save your brother."

"I just don't want you having the easy way out, that's all, not when prison waits for you. And I am not your brother." I hang my head. "I'll never think of you like that again."

"So that's it, you're just going to give up on me, just like that? We made a pact – we'd always have each other's backs."

"I'm just happy I've got a good woman who's worth staying out of prison for – if not, you'd be dead."

He laughs, but quickly the laughter turns to weeping. I don't know whether the realisation has finally hit him of what he really did, or whether he remembers a glimpse of the person he was. Either way, I get to my feet and step over him – he has to live with himself now and I have to find Maddison.

CHAPTER FIFTY-FOUR

MADDISON

I let the blood on my hands get washed away by the rain. My mind is scrambled with so many thoughts at once that it leaves me breathless. I should stop and compose myself, but I keep on running. I don't look back, I just keep running to the ranch. All I have in my head is the piglets, how I need to be there and save them in case they're born. My torn t-shirt clings to me in the rain and the gravel is like a mudslide – it's hard to run on it, like sand on a beach, but I keep going. The adrenaline doesn't allow me to slow down, despite the wind being so harsh against my body.

By the time I get to the ranch everything is chaos – parts of the barn are coming away in the wind, pieces of wood are being flung into the air, the horses are loud and restless, and pieces of hay swirl around me. I cry because the animals are as scared as I am – they're scared of the storm, and I'm scared of what happened and what *almost* happened. I try to reinforce the barn by sliding the locks across, but I don't think it'll help much.

My attention then turns to the pig who is still in the makeshift pen next door. The skies roar above me as I make my way to her.

"No, oh no!" I sob when I see her piglets have been born and they're trying to feed from her. "Please don't die," I cry as I collect as many as I can in my arms and race them to the porch.

As I run back I see Hendrix darting towards me, shouting my name desperately through the wind but I barely hear him. I ignore him and gather up another two piglets and try shielding them in my torn t-shirt. I begin running back with them when Hendrix runs in front of me.

"Maddison, what are you doing?"

"They're going to die if we don't move them!"

"So will you if you don't get into the cellar right now. I saw a tornado headed right this way!" He tugs my arm and tries to lead me to the cellar.

"No! I've got to save them first!" I shout through the chaos, but it's deafening.

Hendrix takes my face into his hands. "Look at me, I need you to be safe."

"Then help me!" I yell. "Help me!"

He shakes his head in frustration for but runs back over to the shelter and rescues the last three piglets. He meets me back at the porch with them and then we collect them all into a basket and carry them to the cellar.

I climb carefully down the steps until we are in a small space with tinned food, flashlights, water and a bed. Hendrix slams shut the cellar door and puts the bolt straight across it. I place the basket of piglets carefully down on the floor.

"Wait, what about their mum?"

Hendrix places his arms around my shoulders. "Listen to me, we don't have time, the tornado is coming and I'm not losing you for a pig."

"But if I go now..."

"No," he cuts me off. "You just want to keep busy because if you stop you have to deal with what just happened. I know that feeling, but you've got to stop, you have to breathe..."

He's still holding me by the shoulders, staring into my eyes, waiting for permission to hug me.

"He nearly..." I choke on my emotions and burst into tears. Hendrix pulls me in and wraps his arms around me, holding me. He doesn't need to say it, I know that he knows what happened, it's written all over his face.

I collapse to the floor and Hendrix copies, allowing me to settle between his thighs. I sit sprawled out between his legs, sobbing into his arms. He rocks me, trying to comfort me, and kisses the top of my head. He doesn't say anything, and he doesn't let go. We stay like this for at least half an hour.

It starts to quieten down outside, and I feel relieved for the animals.

"Hendrix," I whisper, "are you going to prison?"

"What?" He tilts my head to face him. "Why would you say that?"

"You have blood on your knuckles – did you do anything you can't undo?" My heart drops as I wait for the answer. I don't want a life without him.

"I started to, but then I remembered our promise and I stopped myself."

I smile into his chest, relieved.

"Where is he now?"

He shrugs against me. "Jail probably. Adelaide and Pete came to find us to warn us that the tornado was coming, they saw the state of the clinic. Adelaide phoned the police and reported him for attempted ra..." He swallows hard.

"Attempted rape."

I grip his hand in mine. "I hit him in the head with a lamp."

"I saw!" He half laughs. "And I couldn't have been prouder." Just as he plants another kiss on my head, voices start calling us from above.

"Hendrix... Maddison!?"

It's Tucker.

"Down here!" Hendrix calls back, getting up to unlock the door.

"Oh thank God! They're okay!" he calls back to Savannah. "Did you guys see that huge twister? It was wild, one of the biggest I've seen in years!"

"Why are you guys here, I thought you were waiting it out?" Hendrix stares at Savannah who is still clutching her hospital notes to her chest.

"We were, someone said it was over, so we left, then ended up driving along side it!"

Hendrix carefully helps me up.

"Oh wow, the piglets arrived too. What were the chances? Thank you so much for keeping them safe."

"You can thank Maddison and her stubborn ass for that."

Tucker smirks and looks as though he's about to respond with a joke when he catches my torn t-shirt and Hendrix's bloodied hand.

"It's a long story," Hendrix answers before he can ask anything. "And I need to talk to Maddison about it before I can share it with anyone else."

CHAPTER FIFTY-FIVE

HENDRIX

First things first, I run us a shower. I can't bear to look at her torn clothes, knowing he has had his hands on her body.

She looks awkward as she strips off in the bathroom, like she trusts me but still wants to hide her body from me. I turn my back to give her some privacy. I can only imagine how Martinez has left her feeling.

Once she steps into the shower she nods, letting me know it's okay for me to join her. She stands with her back to me, directly under the shower head, letting the water wash him off her skin. I don't rush her; I know she needs this time to feel clean. I pick up a body scrub and apply some body wash to it, letting it foam up in my hands before I gently rub it across her back. She turns to peer at me over her shoulder, giving me a small appreciative look. I drag it carefully across her shoulder blades and down the back of her arms before bringing it back and rubbing it down her spine and across her hips. She lets out a sigh. It's like she's letting the day go with a breath. She leans into me and pulls my arms until they're wrapped around her body.

Slowly, she turns to face me. Her hands trace the tattoos on my chest which seems to be her favourite thing to do. Her eyes look sad, but her body tells me she needs this closeness. I stay with my hands on her hips, following her lead. Eventually her eyes meet mine and she brings her hands up around my neck. I lower my head and she takes the opportunity to kiss me, slowly at first but the passion soon builds. Her tongue finds mine and she lets out a moan against me; her hand grips the back of my head and she leans up on tiptoes until I scoop my arms under her and hoist her up against the tiled wall. She instantly crosses her legs around my waist and smiles, taking this moment in.

The next ten minutes are like nothing I have ever felt before. I hold her against the tiles, kissing her, tasting her, savouring her, trying to take away any hurt. She relaxes into me, enjoying my tenderness I can show her. I kiss every single inch of her as she watches intently, needing my mouth to kiss the day away.

"I love you so much." She whispers as my mouth kisses along her collarbone. I stare up to see her eyes closed this time, she's calmer now than she was, she looks ready to talk.

When I get her out and dry, I light the fire in the bedroom and she sits comfortably in my chair with a blanket draped around her. I perch on the edge of the bed, building up the courage to tell her in detail the things I saw in Afghanistan. I fidget with my hands a bit but I manage to make a start. She winces at the facts I have to say but in her eyes I can see how grateful she is to be able to understand what I've been running from.

She nods and listens and, as I would expect, tears up in some places. I tell her everything Martinez did, followed by every struggle I have had since, including the night I wanted to jump off a bridge. It doesn't seem to scare her, she just listens, taking it all in, learning about me.

Somehow it leads me back to 9/11 and I end up telling her about the word 'Hero' and how every time I hear it, I feel a million emotions and none of them are good. I tell her how angry it makes me that my dad left me. I tell her how he was a Hero but lost everything in the process and so did I. I tell her that I lost it after the school fire because everyone in the town started calling me a hero and it made me panic, that somehow that meant I was going to end up just like my dad and end up letting somebody else down. She listens, deep in thought, trying to keep up with everything I have to say.

"I see it differently," she interjects. "I don't think your dad ran to that building because he was choosing your mom over you, I think he tried to save her for you."

I pause, staring blankly into space.

"Think about it, you said you were really close to your mom and that you were the apple of her eye. So maybe your dad was trying to save her for you. It sounds that way, because no parent runs into a fire knowing they could leave their child an orphan, but they do run into one if they think they can save you from grief."

My eyes swell with emotion and my throat grows thick. I can't speak so I just drop my head into my hands, taking in Maddison's words.

"Baby, nobody knew those buildings were going to collapse." She says it so innocently and sweetly that it brings me to the tears I was trying to avoid.

She slides off the chair and kneels down by my feet, cradling my hands in hers.

"I think he was trying to be *your* hero," she says, wiping a tear gently from my cheek. "And you're mine, you've been my hero since the day I walked into that bar in Nashville. You picked up the pieces of my life, you held me when I needed to feel safe, you've given me back my life and you did it all whilst you were fighting your own demons. That's a kind of bravery you don't find in just anyone. I don't even want to think about where my life would be if I was stuck in England, in the same old rut."

"How can I be your hero? Look what happened with Martinez – that wouldn't have happened if you'd never met me."

"There are bad people everywhere in this world,

unfortunately that part is something we can't control, you know that better than anyone. But being a Hero is about trying, even when it's scary. That's why your dad is a Hero and that is why *you* are mine."

She opens my hands enough so she can slip into my arms, and she holds me tight, letting me know she isn't going anywhere. No matter what comes our way, she's staying.

CHAPTER FIFTY-SIX

MADDISON

The cold autumn air in New York City definitely wakes you up – I can only imagine what it's like in the middle of winter. The golden leaves from the trees have fallen onto the streets, giving it a real splash of colour. I have never been to New York, it's somewhere I only ever saw in the movies, *Home Alone 2* mainly, but it's truly breath-taking. Even though I'm not much of a city girl, I can appreciate how magnificent it is.

Hendrix grips my hand tighter the closer we get to Ground Zero. I think this is the furthest he has made it from what he has told me, and I couldn't be prouder. I don't want to congratulate him yet because I'm fully aware he may turn back around at any time, and I would completely understand. As we approach the memorial, I'm amazed at how two huge skyscrapers were once here, it doesn't look like they could fit in there now. The trees that wrap around the memorial glow that beautiful autumn orange, the grounds are pristine, beautifully kept and respected. That makes me happy straight away for Hendrix, who looks emotional the closer we get. I see his jaw twitch the way it always does when he wants to keep himself composed and strong.

I follow Hendrix quietly as he finds his parents' names. He seems to have an idea where to look, since his grandma used to describe where they were. I listen to the gentle sounds of the waterfall, taking it all in. The atmosphere is calm.

"Here…" he says, pointing at the engraved names, side by side – Dawson Caine & Kimberley Caine, written amongst almost three thousand other names. Hendrix allows his fingers to feel the inscription of their names and looks proud as he does so.

Together we lay one red rose and one white rose beside them. I catch his stare, he looks content, like this has given him the sense of closure he has needed. No more pain, just pride that his parents are being honoured on this beautiful monument. He smiles and kisses me on the forehead.

Smoothly, his hand glides out of his pocket and in front of me is a black velvet box. My jaw drops as he opens it, revealing a white gold princess cut engagement ring.

He doesn't have to say a single thing, his smile says it all. I want him too, forever.

"Yes!" I let out a cry. "I will marry you."

Printed in Great Britain
by Amazon